A NASTY TRICK

"Who . . . who are you?" Kit stammered.

"A pal of the paw, a friend of the fur, all of one claw, and so forth . . . ," said the cat. "Why don't you come up here to this branch, where it's safer from those nasty old hounds."

"I don't know what they want from me," Kit whined. "I think they . . . hurt my parents."

"Hush, little fellow," the cat comforted him. "Come on up here, and we can chat all about it."

Kit glanced down at the howling dogs below and up at the strange cat above. Then he planted his black claws in the bark and hoisted himself up.

"Nice to meet you, guy," the cat said. "What's your name?"

"Kit," Kit said, using his gray-and-black-striped tail to wipe away a tear from the dark fur around his eyes.

"It is good to meet you, Kit. Sixclaw's my name," the cat said. "For obvious reasons."

The cat smiled, and Kit laughed.

"You seem like a nice kid, and it is truly sad when bad things happen to nice kids," Sixclaw added.

The cat sighed. "And of course, sadder still when things seem like they finally might get better but, instead, they get so very, very much worse."

Kit glanced sideways at the cat, whose mouth had opened into a cut-throat grin. Without another word, the cat shoved Kit from the tree.

Kit fell, and as he fell, he heard the dogs below howl with violent glee.

OTHER BOOKS YOU MAY ENJOY

The Call of the Wild (Puffin Classics)	Jack London
Circus Mirandus	Cassie Beasley
The Dark Wild	Piers Torday
James and the Giant Peach	Roald Dahl
The Last Wild	Piers Torday
The Mouse with the Question Mark Tail	Richard Peck
Redwall	Brian Jacques
Secrets at Sea	Richard Peck
The Shadows (The Books of Elsewhere, Volume I)	Jacqueline West
A Tale Dark and Grimm	Adam Gidwitz

Also by C. Alexander London

An Accidental Adventure:
We Are Not Eaten by Yaks
We Dine with Cannibals
We Give a Squid a Wedgie
We Sled with Dragons

Dog Tags:
Semper Fido
Strays
Prisoners of War
Divided We Fall

Tides of War:
Blood in the Water
Honor Bound
Enemy Lines
Endurance

The 39 Clues:
Doublecross Book 2: Mission Hindenburg

THE WILD ONES

C. Alexander London

PUFFIN BOOKS

PUFFIN BOOKS
An imprint of Penguin Random House LLC
375 Hudson Street
New York, New York 10014

First published in the United States of America by Philomel Books,
an imprint of Penguin Group (USA) LLC, 2015
Published by Puffin Books, an imprint of Penguin Random House LLC, 2016

THE LIBRARY OF CONGRESS HAS CATALOGED THE PHILOMEL BOOKS EDITION AS FOLLOWS:
London, C. Alexander, author. The wild ones / C. Alexander London. pages cm.
Summary: After his parents are killed, Kit, a young raccoon, sets off for the
city with a stone that may be the key to finding the Bone of Contention, a legendary
object that is proof of a deal giving the wild animals the rights to Ankle Snap Alley,
which the dogs and cats—known as the Flealess—want back and are willing to kill for.
1. Raccoon—Juvenile fiction. 2. Animals—Juvenile fiction.
3. Quests (Expeditions)—Juvenile fiction. 4. Territoriality (Zoology)—Juvenile fiction.
[1. Raccoon—Fiction. 2. Animals—Fiction. 3. Fantasy.] I. Title.
PZ7.L8419Wi 2015 [Fic]—dc23 2014040349
ISBN: 978-0-399-17099-7 (hardcover)

Puffin Books ISBN 9780147513229

Printed in the United States of America

3 5 7 9 10 8 6 4 2

Edited by Jill Santopolo. Design by Semadar Megged.

To Brian Jacques, whose books made me a reader,
and to Mr. Xanders, who made me read them

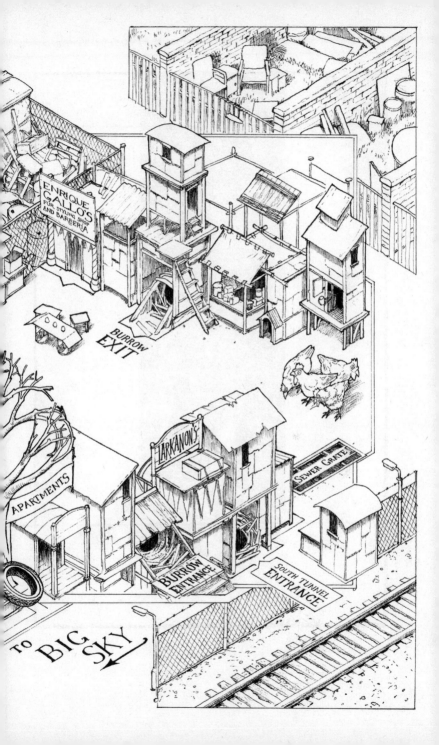

Part I
RACCOON
ON THE RUN

Chapter One

DECENT HOUSE PETS

OF all the alleys beneath the Slivered Sky where the animals of fur and feather make themselves at home, Ankle Snap Alley was the most notorious. It was known far and wide as a den of thieves and crooks and cheats. In Ankle Snap Alley, honest folk were rare as roses in winter, and a decent house pet from a good home would never set foot in such a garbage heap.

And yet, one night, not all that long ago, a whisper-thin silver dog came creeping into the winding paths of the alley. The dog was a miniature greyhound. He stepped daintily across the broken concrete, hopped over weed-choked trash, and skirted the rusted skeleton of a bicycle, which he glanced at with disgust.

The dog's collar was fine leather, and two jingling tags hung off it. One tag said he'd had all his shots from the veterinarian, and the other gave the address of the home where his People fed him and bathed him and invited him to sleep at the foot of their soft feather bed.

The dog froze in place, lifted one paw from the earth, and sniffed at the moon-kissed air. He swiveled his thin neck around and saw a glint of yellow eyes in the shadow between two buildings. A tiny bell made a delicate tinkling noise. The jingle of the dog's tags answered the bell. That was the signal. The dog was in the right place.

"Do you have information for me?" he asked the shadowy figure. Although the miniature greyhound's body was dainty, his voice was deep and rumbling, like dynamite in a silk purse.

Two yellow eyes blazed from the shadows. "Me?" the other creature replied. "No, I do not."

The dog snarled. "How dare you call me out here at this undogly hour and waste my time with no information."

"Listen more carefully, Titus," hissed the creature in the shadows. "I said *I* don't have information for you. But *he* does."

There was a flash of orange claw as the figure shoved a

small animal from the shadows into a puddle of moonlight. It was a black-and-white woodpecker with a shock of red plumage atop its head. It looked about frantically. The little bird's wings were bound to its body by a rubber band, and a metal paper clip clamped its beak shut. One of the bird's eyes was swollen shut, and it hopped forward with a distinct limp.

"He took some *convincing*," the shadowy figure said. "But I promised if he talked I wouldn't eat his head."

The bird squealed through his clamped beak.

"Now tell him what you told me," the creature ordered the bird. "Have they found the Bone of Contention?"

The bird shook his head no. The dog exhaled with relief.

"But they've found a clue," said the figure in the shadows. "He saw 'em buy a stone from a traveling deer. It had the markings of Azban, the First Raccoon, on it. Isn't that so?"

The bird nodded yes.

The dog sighed. "So they're closer than ever to finding the Bone?"

"If you believe the Bone is real," said the shadowy voice. "Cats don't put much faith in the old stories."

"You cats were wild in the old days," said Titus. "We dogs were not. We know the Bone of Contention is real. And that is why it must never be found." The dog narrowed his eyes at the woodpecker. "Tell me, bird, where do they live?"

"Mrrpm, mrrm, mrrrp," said the bird through his clipped beak.

"Hush," said the dog. "Don't talk." He slid a piece of tree bark forward on the ground and placed it directly beneath the bird in the white moonlight. "Write."

The bird bent its head and pecked at the bark on the ground; the *tap-tap-tap* of its beak echoed in the quiet. When it was done, the dog looked at the address the woodpecker had pecked.

"Thank you," he said. Then he spoke to the yellow-eyed shadow. "Sixclaw, you'll take care of them?"

The figure in the shadows laughed. "You dogs never say what you mean. 'Take *care* of them'?"

"You know what I mean."

"You want them dead?"

"I want them dead," Titus agreed. "No one can ever find the Bone of Contention. Especially not the stinking raccoons, not their stinking children, not their children's children . . . who I am certain will also stink."

The creature stepped from the shadow into the circle of moonlight beside the captive woodpecker. He was an orange-and-white cat wearing a purple collar on which hung a small bell that chimed every time he moved. "My services do not come cheap," he said.

"When the job is done, you'll get more than you could ever desire," Titus said.

"I can desire a lot," Sixclaw answered. "A cat's appetites are bottomless."

"Well, you can whet your appetite with this little bird here," said Titus. The bird's eyes widened, and the cat grinned from ear to ear. His pink tongue danced across his razor-sharp teeth.

Titus turned to go, picking his way back over the strewn garbage and overgrown grass of the alley, cautious with every placement of his paws. He hated to visit this filthy place and hated to do business with cats like Sixclaw, who were half wild in spite of their collars and dishes of milk left out on porches. Sometimes unpleasant alliances were necessary, even between cats and dogs. They were on the same side after all, when it came to ridding themselves of the vermin of Ankle Snap Alley.

As he left the cat and his prey behind, he turned his head back with a jingle of dog tags. "When you eat the bird, leave his head for the vermin to find," he called back. "As a warning from the Flealess. Their time is up."

Chapter Two

RACCOON RUN

RUN! Kit scrambled on all four paws, charging across the field for the tree line. The big sky above was bright blue, and the sun blazed yellow with the glare of day. He had been woken from a deep sleep in his burrow, and now a pack of hunting dogs howled and snarled on his heels.

They had his scent, five of them, all bred to kill. They could outrun a fox or a rabbit, and they could certainly outrun a woodland raccoon like Kit. He'd never been chased before; he didn't know what to do.

His instincts screamed at him to move and to move fast, while his mind raced to catch up with his body.

In his head, his mother's shout echoed. "Kit! Wake up! They're here for us! Run!"

His lungs burned, his legs ached, but he ran as fast as he could. Why were they chasing him? And what had they done to his parents?

"Keeping running, lad," the leader of the pack of dogs called out. "It'll be that much more fun when we tear you to pieces."

The other dogs howled and jeered. He could smell their hot breath. His senses prickled, and he dared a glance over his shoulder.

They were nearly on him!

The massive bloodhounds wore thick leather collars. Their brown ears fluttered like banners, their fangs glistened with slobber. The leader of the pack snapped and nearly caught Kit's tail.

He couldn't outrun them.

But he was a raccoon, was he not? Cleverest of the animals, his father always said, a son of Azban, the First Raccoon, who could've tricked the light from the moon if he'd wanted to. Kit couldn't outrun these brutes, but he could outthink them.

What did he know about dogs? What could he do that they couldn't?

An idea slapped him like a branch across the face: He could climb.

He turned sharply, leaping sideways just as the pack leader dove to bite again. The dog's jaws clamped around nothing but grass, and the other dogs tumbled into him from behind, rolling on top of one another in a snarly heap. Kit bolted hard for the nearest tree at the edge of the meadow.

The dogs were on their feet again. He'd cut the distance to the tree in half, but the pack was cutting the distance between them faster. He didn't know if he would make it. The thought of dogs' teeth breaking his fur and gnawing at his bones added speed to his stride. When he reached the tree, he jumped for the trunk and caught on with his claws. He scampered up, catching his breath in the crook of the first branch he grabbed.

The dogs circled the base of the tree, barking mad.

"You get down here and face your doom," the pack leader demanded.

"Go away," Kit shouted down at them. "Leave me alone!"

The dogs laughed uproariously at that. One of them laughed so hard he had to lie down and roll on his back, his snout rubbing into the dirt.

"Look, little guy, it's nothing personal," the pack leader explained. "We've been hired to do a job of killing you, so that's what we've got to do. You come on down and get killed, and that'll be that. I promise, we'll do it quick. It won't hurt . . . much. We won't even eat your head."

Kit scooted higher up into the tree, so high that the dogs below looked small as mice. He curled into a ball in the safe crook of a branch and shuddered. The dogs paced, waiting for him to tire. But Kit could stay up in the tree for days. The dogs would go eventually. They had collars on; they were People's dogs. They couldn't wait for him forever, could they? Would they?

And, still, the question rattled his mind, *Why?*

It had been a beautiful night, the night before. Stars blooming across the sky as thick as thorn bushes and a moon so round and bright it put the daytime sun to shame.

Kit's family burrow was a cozy place, with a nice hole under their big tree to enter through, a great room where his mother and father worked on their archeological discoveries together, while Kit would play outside.

That night, Kit had played in the moonlight with some of the rabbits from the tree next door, showing them how to tie and untie knots in blades of grass. The rabbits were hopeless at it, but they enjoyed watching Kit's nimble fingers.

His mother made an apple grub cake for dinner, while his father studied a strange piece of stone he'd brought back from one of his foraging trips in the city beneath the Slivered Sky.

Kit, being a Big Sky raccoon, was not allowed to accompany his parents on these trips to the city, where the

People's tall buildings cut the sky into slivers, but he loved hearing tales of the goings-on.

"The city's a rough and unforgiving place," his father explained to him. "If it isn't People trying to trap and kill wild folk like us, it's their terrible house pets hunting us down for sport. Even the other wild animals scheme and plot to take what doesn't belong to them. It's a brutish life in the city, Kit, and you're better off out here in woodlands beneath the Big Sky."

"But doesn't Uncle Rik live in the city?" Kit asked.

"Your mother's brother does live there," said Kit's father. "He's more comfortable surrounded by no-good garbage-scrounging liars than your mother and I are."

"Is that why I've never met Uncle Rik?" Kit wondered.

"He's got important work to do in the city," Kit's mother told him. "And we've got important work here. I'm sure you'll meet him one day."

His father returned to studying the piece of stone in his paws. It was perfectly flat on one side, with jagged edges, like it'd been broken off from something bigger. On it there was a paw print, which Kit's parents told him was how the First Animals wrote.

"Did you find that in the city?" Kit asked.

"Not quite." His father sighed. "I bought it off a traveling deer, who bought it off a nervous gopher, who says he bought it off a hedgehog in a shop beneath the Slivered Sky. I recognized the footprint right away. Azban, the First Raccoon."

"What's it say?" Kit asked.

"I've no idea," said his father. "Your mother's the one who reads the old language."

"Hey, Ma," Kit called. "What's this old stone say?"

"I don't know, my son," she told him. "I've been too busy making your dinner to study it properly yet. Perhaps if you learned to cook, instead of playing with knots, then I'd have more time to do my work—"

"Don't let the boy cook!" his father cried out. "We'll be eating acorn candy and honeycomb pie for every meal."

The whole family laughed. Kit really loved acorn candy and honeycomb pie.

After dinner, his parents tucked him into his burrow, smoothing the soft moss and letting him nuzzle in their fur.

His mother told him a story, a story of Azban, the First Raccoon, who had tricked Brutus, Duke of Dogs, in a game of chance and won the moonlight from him. From that time on, the People's house pets, the Flealess, were banished to the bright and terrible day. Only the Wild Ones were left free to romp and howl in the cool moonlight as they pleased.

"That's why the Flealess won't leave our kind in

peace," his mother told him. "They want the moonlight back. They think we cheated it from them."

"But we didn't, did we, Ma?" Kit asked. "It's just a story, right?"

"You can't steal what is freely given," his mother told him. "Azban was too clever to cheat. I imagine the truth is he won a game fair and square, and the Flealess are just looking to old stories for an excuse to why they hate our kind . . . but don't you worry about that." She patted his head. "Out here in the Big Sky there are no Flealess to fret over. It's a nice place to live, isn't it?"

"It is," Kit agreed and drifted off to sleep just as the sun came up, glad for Azban and the blessed moonlight . . . and then:

HOWL! CRASH! SHRIEK!

The dogs burst into the raccoon warren. His father was already fighting them in the other room as Kit's mother jostled him awake. She shoved his arms into his jacket, flopped a hat onto his head, and stuffed a pouch of nuts and seeds—emergency money—into his pocket. She told him to run.

She didn't say why or who from or where to.

And now, here he was, confused and frightened, alone up a tree, a raccoon on the run.

. . .

"Tough spot, huh, kiddo." Startled by the unexpected voice, Kit nearly fell out of the nook of his branch. He heard the dinging of a tiny bell. "Relax," said the voice. "I'm a friend of the fur."

Kit looked up and saw a bright orange cat with blazing yellow eyes perched on a branch above him. The cat wore a purple collar with a bell on it. The breeze through the tree made the bell chime quietly. It was almost soothing.

Kit's nose worked the air, confused. The cat had the smell of the Flealess—shampoos and People and their fancy foods—but there were no People in this wood, save the hunters and their dogs.

"Who . . . who are you?" Kit stammered.

"A pal of the paw, a friend of the fur, all of one claw, and so forth . . . ," said the cat. "Why don't you come up here to this branch, where it's safer from those nasty old hounds."

"I don't know what they want from me," Kit whined. "I think they . . . hurt my parents."

"Hush, little fellow," the cat comforted him. "Come on up here, and we can chat all about it."

Kit glanced down at the howling dogs below and up at the strange cat above. Then he planted his black claws in the bark and hoisted himself up.

"Nice to meet you, guy," the cat said. "What's your name?"

"Kit," Kit said, using his gray-and-black-striped tail to wipe away a tear from the dark fur around his eyes.

The cat put a paw on Kit's shoulder. Kit noticed the cat had six claws on his paws, instead of the usual five. He felt the prickly sensation as the tips of each razor-sharp claw rested against his fur.

"It is good to meet you, Kit. Sixclaw's my name," the cat said. "For obvious reasons."

The cat smiled, and Kit laughed.

"You seem like a nice kid, and it is truly sad when bad things happen to nice kids," Sixclaw added.

Kit nodded.

The cat sighed. "And of course, sadder still is when things seem like they finally might get better but, instead, they get so very, very much worse."

Kit glanced sideways at the cat, whose mouth had opened into a cut-throat grin. Without another word, the cat shoved Kit from the tree.

Kit fell, and as he fell, he heard the dogs below howl with violent glee.

"Nice one, Sixclaw!" the pack leader shouted, just before Kit hit the ground with a wind-thumping thud.

Chapter Three

THE SHORT
GOOD-BYE

KIT heaved for breath and looked up at the cruel faces of five bloodhounds circled around him. Above them, peering down from the tree, was the bright orange cat, fur blazing against the blue sky like another furious sun. Oh, how Kit longed for the cool moonlight and the safety of his family's burrow!

"Have fun, fellas," the cat called down to the dogs. "Remember, I don't get paid until he's torn to pieces, so *you* don't get paid until he's torn to pieces."

Kit winced. The dogs rumbled out low growls and squeezed the circle in tighter.

"Wait!" the cat cried. Maybe, Kit thought, the cat had realized his mistake. Maybe he had realized that he had the wrong raccoon, that he and his parents had no quarrel with anyone, let alone a bunch of Flealess cats and dogs. They were just simple woodland raccoons living under the Big Sky and not bothering anyone of fur or feather, beak or claw, wing or wattle. Maybe the dogs would let him go home now with an apology and a pat on the back, and he and his parents would be laughing about the mix-up by sunset.

"Don't eat the head," the cat shouted, as he strolled back along the branch. "Boss likes to leave the heads."

The cat skulked away along the highway of tree branches and disappeared into the green and gold canopy of leaves. The dogs resumed their growling, and Kit's heart sank.

"You should've come down sooner," the pack leader told him. "Now I gotta make it hurt. I think I'll tear your head off myself."

"I'll take the tail!" another dog shouted, leaping forward.

"Tug-o'-war, tug-o'-war, tug-o'-war," the dogs chanted.

Dogs, it was well known, loved nothing more than a vicious game of tug-o'-war.

Just as the pack leader jumped at Kit, there was a flash of gray-and-black fur, a sudden yelp, and the dog was flung sideways, hitting the dirt upside down. His legs kicked wildly at the air as he struggled to roll himself off his back and get to his feet again.

"Leave my boy alone!" Kit's mother shouted, as she assumed a fighting stance on her back paws between the dogs and Kit.

"Rrrrr!" growled the pack leader. "I thought we killed you already. Give us Azban's Footprint, and we won't kill your boy like we did your husband."

"Dad?" Kit cried out from behind his mother. She kept her eyes locked on the dogs. There would be time for sadness later. Right now, escape for her son was her only concern.

"That's a nice bark you've got," she snarled at the dog. "I bet it's much worse than your bite."

The dog, enraged, jumped at Kit's mother again. Two others flanked her.

Kit's mother sidestepped them carefully, hooking her paw into the leader's collar as he dove and using his own speed to swing him into the other two dogs. All of them hit the ground hard and tangled into one another. With her back claw, his mother slashed the pack leader's ankle, changing his growls to yelps.

Kit marveled that his mother knew how to fight

claw-jitsu. It was like she had this whole secret life he knew nothing about.

"Kit, watch out!" she warned, as the remaining two dogs came at him. He dodged their first bite, then spun around the trunk of the tree. They chased him in circles.

"Stop!" the leader called out.

The dogs stopped chasing Kit. Kit stopped running. He looked back to see his mother holding the pack leader's collar. With every twist of her paw, the dog's collar got tighter, choking him.

"Let my son go," Kit's mother ordered. "Or your leader gets collared."

The dogs hesitated. Their leader whimpered.

"I'm warning you," Kit's mother said. "I'm no scared country mama. I was born in Ankle Snap Alley, and I can fight as dirty as any dog."

"Back off, boys," the pack leader choked out, and the dogs stepped away from Kit.

"Roll on your backs," Kit's mother ordered, and the dogs all obeyed. "And, Kit," she spoke to him. "When I say so, run."

Kit nodded.

For one heavy moment all was silent and still as a forest in snowfall. Kit's mother twisted the dog's collar until his eyes bulged, then she broke the deadly silence with a shout: "Run!"

She dove from atop the hound dog and leaped all the way to the tree where Kit stood. Grabbing Kit by the paw, she pulled him along with her. It took the pack leader another moment before he could speak again, and another moment for the confused pack of dogs to roll off their backs in the dirt, sniff out which direction the raccoons had gone, and follow their boss's orders, which were simple enough: "Get them!"

The pack leader limped along behind, though none of the dogs was running quite as fast as he had before. Getting beaten up by a mama raccoon hurt their pride as much as their hides, and a dog's wounded pride could slow him down worse than a wounded leg.

Kit and his mother ran as fast as they could.

"This isn't the way home," Kit panted.

"We can't go home," Kit's mother replied. "They know where we live. We're going to the city under the Slivered Sky to find your uncle."

"Uncle Rik?" Kit asked. "But I thought he lived around a bunch of no-good garbage-scrounging liars?"

His mother didn't answer. She just kept pulling him along, running.

"I didn't know you were from there," Kit added.

The dogs barked after them in the distance, catching up, but not fast enough. There was a river up ahead and tree branches that hung over it. The raccoons could climb and leap across to where the dogs couldn't follow. They'd be safe on the other side.

It looked like they were going to make it, when there was a loud *SNAP!*

Kit felt his mother's hand jerk out of his, and she fell backward. He skittered to a stop and turned around. She'd stepped into a metal trap that was hidden beneath a pile of leaves. It was a small tube on the end of a chain and her back paw was stuck in it. When she tried to pull her paw out, the trap tightened on her ankle. The more she tugged, the tighter the trap locked around her paw. Her front paws tugged at the tube, but she couldn't loosen it. The dogs barked and howled, ever closer.

"Mom!" Kit gripped the chain, tugged, shook it.

"You need to go, Kit," his mother said. "Leave me. Run."

"Why is this happening?" Kit asked her. "I don't understand."

His mother pulled out the flat stone that his father had been studying. It was crumbling, but had the paw print of the raccoon and a smear of colorful paint on it, a broken piece of a much larger picture. "Give this to your uncle Rik," she said. "He'll know what to do with it. It's important that he get this stone. It could help prevent a terrible war. The fate of countless creatures depends on it."

She stuffed it into his pocket.

"You give it to him yourself, Ma." Kit shook his head and studied the mechanism. "I can open this."

He knew he was good with traps and locks. He followed the chain paw over paw to a stake that held it in place. He tried lifting the stake, heaving it with all his strength, but it was buried too deep. He started to dig up the dirt around it, but the ground was hard and the digging was too slow. The dogs were getting closer. He ran back to his mother, studied her ankle where it vanished into the metal tube. A metal snapping lever locked the trap shut around her paw. If Kit could pry back the lever, she could slip out.

The dogs' barks grew louder.

Kit's little paws worried at the lever, lifting it ever so delicately. It wouldn't budge. He had to find something to pry it open with.

"Kit. There's no time."

"There *is* time! I can do this," he objected. He scrounged for a stick, but it broke the moment he jammed it into the lever. He needed something stronger. He searched again.

"No, son," his mother said. "You have to run. You have to get that stone to your uncle. That is a Footprint of Azban, the First Raccoon."

"So what? I can't leave you," Kit pleaded.

"Your father and I—" His mother's voice cracked in her throat. "We'll always be with you." With her free paws, she embraced Kit. "But you must find your uncle Rik. You must help him finish the work we've begun."

"How do I find him?" Kit's voice quivered. "I've never been to the city."

His mother bent down and jabbed her claw into one of the pokeberries that littered the forest floor and she scratched an address in black juice onto a thin piece of birch bark. "Watch out when you get there," she warned Kit. "His neighborhood really is filled with no-good down-and-out garbage-scrounging liars. Be careful."

"But I want you to come—" He held up the big stick he'd found.

"No," said his mother. "You have to go now."

The dogs bounded over the top of a nearby ridge. They stopped and scanned the woods, pausing a moment before locking their noses onto Kit and his mother.

"Got 'em!" one dog shouted.

"Grow up brave and quick of paw, Kit," his mother pleaded. "Kind to your family and true to your friends."

Kit hesitated. The dogs charged.

"Run!" his mother shouted one final time, and Kit dropped the big stick in front of her and backed away. Before he turned to run, he touched the tips of his claws together, forming the shape of the letter A with his paws, the raccoon sign of greeting and good-bye, the sign for Azban, the First Raccoon. The sign of trust.

His mother matched the gesture. She trusted him to carry on, to find his uncle, and to grow up on his own. This was good-bye.

Kit turned and ran for the river as the dogs pounced on his mother. He didn't listen as they attacked nor as she shouted, "Is that all you got, you lousy leash lovers!"

He headed straightaway for the city under the Slivered Sky, and an uncle he had never met. His mother said that he now carried the fate of countless creatures in the patch-work pocket of his little coat.

He still didn't know why.

Part II

LIARS, CHEATS, AND UNCLES

Chapter Four

AN HONEST FELLOW

JUST as the sky was settling into dusk, when the shadows pulled the dark curtain down on the day, Kit arrived in Ankle Snap Alley. He wore his hat low over his ears and flipped up the collar of his coat. He thought it gave him a tough guy look, something to make no-good garbage-scrounging liars wary, should he encounter any on his way.

Even though he'd been traveling for a day and a night and another whole day, he still had the smell of moss on him, and of dirt and bark. Big Sky smells. He was no city fellow, that was plain, and he sniffed warily at the evening air.

He did not belong here.

The buildings on either side of the alley carved a narrow ribbon overhead, blocking the view of the moon and stars, which is how the city got the name of Slivered Sky. Kit was from out where the sky was as big as seeing, and he had never set paw in any city before. His senses prickled.

His black-striped tail curled around his side as he leaned back on his haunches to study the piece of bark he clutched in his paw. The writing made him wince at the memory of the writer. He tapped the seed pouch in his front pocket to make sure his savings were safe. He'd moved Azban's Footprint into the pouch so that he wouldn't lose it. The mysterious object felt heavy and important, and he was eager to give it to his uncle and find out what it meant and why the Flealess would attack his parents for it. What did they care about Azban's Footprint anyway? It was just a historical raccoon artifact, the kind his mom and dad had always collected. What made this one so important?

He'd carried the strange stone here all the way through woodlands and People's neighborhoods and across a great green bridge where giant metal cars sped and honked, and the People in them didn't even look in his direction. If he hadn't watched his step, they might have run him over.

People thought their civilization was the only one that counted and didn't notice much that went on in the smaller places of the world. They didn't pay any attention to the lives of those furry creatures scurrying beneath them, unless they'd turned them into house pets.

In the old stories, People and animals were all one civilization. They spoke one another's languages and knew one another's ways. It wouldn't have been a strange thing at all to see a raccoon in a hat and coat strolling across a bridge, but they'd all forgotten each other now, and the People's talk sounded to Kit like nothing but mumbles, grunts, and grumbles, and their comings and goings didn't matter much to him. He figured his didn't matter much to them either.

He was on the lookout for the other animals like himself.

Still as a stone, he stood beside an old metal fence that blocked a drop-off beside the tunnel down to metal tracks where the underground trains of the People roared in and out day and night.

Kit stepped away from the fence, unsure which way to go. There was a grate in the ground beside him, and he heard the trickle of water in the dark somewhere on the other side of it, an underwater river of some kind. A sniff told him the river was filled with the runoff waste of all the city, and lingering beneath those smells were other smells, of fear and of death. He backed away from the grate and stumbled into a grumpy mole in a hardhat and dark welding glasses.

"Outta the way, youse!" the mole shouted. "You want to get tossed in the sewers?"

"I . . . no . . . I . . ." Kit mumbled, just as a brown rabbit in a tattered brown suit hopped right into his back, knocking him aside.

"Move it, boy!" said the rabbit without stopping.

Ankle Snap Alley was stirring to life for the night, and nothing stood still for long.

Every kind of creature imaginable made a home in Ankle Snap Alley, the only requirement being that they had nowhere else to go. Down-on-their-luck foxes lived in burrows beside half-crazy rabbits and retired hens, who lived on top of pious church mice and orphaned rats. There were lizards for landlords and possums for grocers, and raccoons mucking about in it all, looking for an easy score, as raccoons have done since the time of Azban, the First Raccoon.

The church mice in their robes handed out pamphlets, the moles rushed to their long shifts of digging and fixing in the dirt, while mean-eyed strays kept on the lookout for trouble or the opportunity to cause some.

As Kit watched, Possum Ansel opened his bakery for the night, filling the alley with the smell of sweetened acorn biscuits, fishbone cookies, and garbage-gristle fried pies. The possum already had a line of customers that wrapped around the corner. They gaped wide-eyed at his sweet confections.

A sleek python, with brown and black scales decorating his long body, slid up to the bakery door. The other creatures looked away as the possum tensed.

"Payment'ssss due, Ansssssel," the python said. "For your protection. Wouldn't want to sssseee anything unfortunate happen to your bussssinessss."

The possum frowned, but gave the snake a bag of seeds, which the big python swallowed whole, then moved on to the next door, which was Enrique Gallo's Fur Styling Shop and Barbería. Enrique, a retired fighting rooster, had filled his shop windows with pictures of his old days in the fighting ring. He paid the snake too, then swung around his sign, and opened his shop for the night. He watched the snake slither away to shake down the next business for a payoff and he shook his head, before strutting silently inside.

Neither the snake nor the possum nor the rooster paid Kit any mind. No one noticed him at all . . . no one except the Blacktail brothers, who'd caught the young raccoon's scent right away.

Raccoons themselves, Shane and Flynn Blacktail had a keen nose for when one of their own arrived in the alley.

"Look of the Big Sky on that one," said Shane to his brother.

"Doesn't know his way around beneath our sliver of sky with its alleys and pavements," Flynn responded.

"He's used to the woods and grasses of the wide-open spaces, I bet you."

"No bet there, my brother. We are in perfect agreement."

"And are we in perfect agreement that a newcomer here, and a pal of our own paw at that, might be needing friends?"

"We are." Flynn nodded. "Friends are what that lad needs, and friends are what we could be."

"Best of friends."

"Oh yes, best friends," said Flynn. "A friend in need, after all, is a friend indeed."

The Blacktail brothers ran a shell-and-nut game—one nut, three shells, and the players try to guess which shell the nut is hidden under. Guess right, the nut's yours. Guess wrong, it'll cost you a nut or a seed or whatever else your pockets might hold.

Many a traveler, rat and raccoon, bird and bunny alike, had emptied his pockets down to dust at the hands of these two Blacktail brothers, who used the word *friend* when they really meant *sucker*.

With a wink, Flynn Blacktail told his brother to start the ballyhoo, that carnival call they used to bring players to their corner game, although they weren't interested in any old player.

No, they had their eyes on the young raccoon, who looked like a "friend" indeed.

Chapter Five

FRIENDS OF THE FUR

YOU *may have luck, you may have plenty!"* Shane Blacktail cried out.

"Five'll get you ten, ten'll get you twenty!" Flynn Blacktail responded right after.

They spoke loud and clear, so loud the whole alley could hear, but their words were meant for Kit alone.

"The game itself is lots of fun," Shane sang. *"A simple bet, pays two to one!"*

"You there! Fine lad!" Flynn called. "Come over here, why don't you?"

The young raccoon looked left and he looked right, certain these two fast-talking corner boys couldn't be speaking to him. He didn't know anyone in this alley. He glanced down at the scrap of bark in his fist. He shuddered at the memory of the dogs pouncing on his mother as he fled, then wiped a single tear from his fur and told his memories to be quiet.

He decided there could be no harm in asking fellow raccoons to point him on his way toward his uncle. They looked friendly enough.

Kit shuffled on over to the twins and sat up on his back paws to greet them with his fingertips touching in an A. They returned the greeting, and he was glad to know that raccoons under the Slivered Sky greeted one another the same way as raccoons did back home. At least one thing about this place was familiar.

The Blacktail brothers smirked from the corners of their mouths. Shane brushed some dirt from his pin-striped pants, and Flynn rolled up the sleeves of his open black shirt.

"What's your name, boy?" Flynn asked.

"Kit," Kit answered.

"A fine name, Kit is," Shane Blacktail said. "This your first time beneath the Slivered Sky, Kit?"

"It is," said Kit.

"Must be hard, not knowing a hide in this town," asked Flynn.

"I have an uncle," Kit explained. "He's supposed to live around here. I'm trying to find him."

He stretched out the piece of bark and Flynn took it casually from him, passing it to his brother without looking at it. Shane set it down on his side of the table, his claw covering it just enough so that Kit couldn't take it back.

"Oh, plenty of time for addresses and uncles," said Flynn. "How about a friendly game to welcome you to the neighborhood?"

"I don't have time for games," said Kit. "I really need to find my uncle."

"But we're practically cousins," said Shane. "Pals of the paw, all of one fur, and so on. All raccoons are cousins, you know? And where there are cousins, uncles are bound to be before long. Ankle Snap's lousy with uncles."

"Lousy with lice too," Flynn added.

"Ankle Snap?" Kit asked them.

"Why that's where you are, young Kit!" Shane laughed. "Ankle Snap Alley."

"Young Kit doesn't know where he is," Flynn mused. "Makes a raccoon wonder how he can know where he's going?"

"We can't have a kid like Kit wandering about the Ankle Snap without knowing where he's going," Shane replied.

"He could end up anywhere," warned Flynn.

"He could end up nowhere!" cried Shane.

"Nowhere, indeed, which also spells Now Here," said Flynn.

"And yet, here he is now," said Shane.

"And now that he *is* here, we can't let him end up nowhere," Flynn agreed.

"Wouldn't be right," Shane concurred.

"Wouldn't be friendly," Flynn amended.

"Wouldn't be . . . *safe*," Shane declared.

The raccoon brothers had a way of bantering so fast it made Kit's head spin, but he caught on to that last word and interrupted their twirling tongues with an alarmed question of his own: *"Safe?"*

"Oh"—Flynn shook his head, sucked air through his teeth—"the Ankle Snap's not safe at all for those who don't know their way."

"Gets its name from the ankle-snapping traps that the People leave about," said Shane. He said the word *People* as if it were a curse word.

"People," Kit echoed, spitting the word out like a curse word too, which made the Blacktail brothers laugh.

"New traps pop up all the time," continued Shane. "People put 'em out while we're sleeping, rearrange them under cover of sunlight. And then of course, they send their house pets out to savor whoever gets stuck inside come sunup."

"Savor?" Kit swallowed.

"To eat!" Flynn laughed. "The Flealess'd eat us all up if they could. Of course, it's easy enough to get around the alley if you've got friends looking out for you."

"Friends to keep you from getting hurt," added Shane.

"And we, as upstanding representatives of the Rabid Rascals," said Flynn, "do not want to see you get hurt."

Now Kit was really confused. "Rabid who?"

Shane shook his head. "He doesn't know the Rabid Rascals."

Flynn nodded kindly. "The Rabid Rascals are a neighborhood watch," he explained. "We're a cohort, if you will, of creatures committed to the safety and well-being of all the residents of Ankle Snap Alley."

"A cohort?" Kit scratched his head. Something didn't sound right. He knew the word *cohort* meant a group, but he began to feel uneasy about how the Blacktail brothers were using the word, as if they meant far more than they said.

"Well," added Shane with a shrug, "some might call us a gang. But we only gang up on folks who don't appreciate our protection. Folks that threaten the safety of our neighborhood."

"And its well-being," added Flynn.

"Of course," said Shane. "We are very committed to well-being, as well as being well."

"Oh yes, *being* well most of all," said Flynn. "And in

the interest of *your* being well, Kit, I suggest you stick with us and play a game or three. I bet you crumbs to nuts that this uncle of yours finds his way to you before the sun comes up again on Ankle Snap."

"I don't think I should be . . . gambling," said Kit.

"Just until an uncle comes along," said Shane. "Uncles are drawn to the old shell game like church mice to peanuts."

Both raccoons looked across the alley at a cluster of three mice taking up the narrow path between P. Ansel's Sweet & Best-Tasting Baking Company and a coop of chickens, settling in to their evening gossip outside the rooster's barbershop. Passersby of all families and furs tried to sidestep the mice, but the little guys got right in the way of cat and rat alike.

"Do you believe peace is possible?" a mouse demanded of a wobbly-looking skunk, shoving a bark pamphlet in his face. "Do you have faith the Wild Ones and the Flealess can live in harmony? We do! We know the way to peace and prosperity!"

The skunk waved him off, staggered around him, and quickly vanished into the dark doorway of a place called Larkanon's, where a mangy dog dozed by the door.

"Morning, Rocks," the skunk said as he tossed the dog a few seeds. The dog put them in a pocket of his jacket and grunted without lifting his head.

The mouse with the pamphlet looked sadly after

the skunk, sighed, and returned to calling out for other passersby. "All the families of fur and feather, paw and claw, predator and prey, all can live in harmony! We needn't pay the Rascals for protection! We needn't fear the Flealess! The woodpecker's fate need not be ours! When the Bone of Contention is found, peace will be at hand!"

"Oh, stuff your cheese holes!" Flynn shouted at the mouse, his fangs flashing. The mouse ignored him completely.

"What's the Bone of Contention?" Kit wondered.

"Don't mind about those church mice and their fables, Kit." Flynn captured his attention once more, all smiles. "You know the game, shells-and-nuts?"

"I . . . uh . . . ," Kit mustered.

"You got any seeds in that fine coat of yours?"

"Well . . . I have seeds, but I really shouldn't . . . I wouldn't want to—"

"If we all lived by shoulds, we wouldn't do a thing worth doing!" Shane cut him off. "Seeds are meant for spending, not for shoulding about in pockets!"

Kit was still puzzling out what *shoulding* could possibly be, but Flynn talked right over his thinking. "We'll put down one nut to four seeds, how about that? You won't find more generous terms in any alley this side of the Slivered Sky. Now, how do those odds sound?"

"Uh . . ." Kit fidgeted nervously. "I don't know what you're saying, really. It is pretty odd."

"Well put, young lad!" Flynn patted him on the back, laughing. "Well put! We've given you odd odds and odd words. What good are words, when the odds are so odd, am I right? Actions speak! Begin, brother. Young Kit here has no use of odd words. But of the odds, he has our word!"

"I . . . what?" Kit was bewildered, but Shane picked up a small nut in his delicate black claw and placed it on a scrap of old cardboard laid across two empty red cans from a toss-away fizzy drink. He laid out three walnut shells and then put the nut beneath one. Then his hands slid and slipped around the table, mixing up the shells.

As Shane's paws moved, Flynn talked, and Flynn's talk was more like a song. He sang:

> *It's a simple game of ifs and buts,*
> *of shells and nuts.*
> *You pick a shell, you try your luck.*
> *Select a shell, the one you choose.*
> *If right, you win, if wrong, you lose.*

Shane's hands sped up; the shells moved faster and faster. Kit thought he knew where the nut was one second; the next he started to doubt. His eyes couldn't keep up with the moving paws, but his ears perked. Even with all the racket of Ankle Snap Alley, he could hear a small knocking sound. It was the sound of the nut knocking against the side of the shell. If he could follow that sound, he could find the nut. That was why Flynn sang . . . to distract the ears of the players!

The luck itself, it comes from you
or from Azban, if saints be true.
The eye won't lie, or will it, so?
You find the nut, and then you'll know!

Kit did his best to ignore the song and listened for the sound of the nut.

Shane stopped moving the shells and lifted his hands away with open palms. As he stopped, Kit's keen ears picked up the sound of the nut under the farthest shell. It wasn't where he'd thought it would be, but he trusted his ears far more than his eyes.

"It's there!" He pointed triumphantly. "It's under that shell."

"You're certain?" Flynn asked him.

Kit nodded to Flynn and Flynn nodded to Shane and Shane tipped the shell back to reveal the nut exactly where Kit had said it would be.

"Winner, winner, nuts for dinner!" Shane called out and Kit felt a rush of excitement. A crowd around him cheered. He hadn't even noticed a crowd gather.

"Nicely done, pal o' me paw," said Flynn. "You've a knack for the game, like all of our kind. He rolled a nut toward Kit, then stopped it with the tip of one claw just as Kit reached out for it. "What say you give a friend, a cousin like meself, a chance to win it back?"

"I don't know," said Kit, who thought it best to quit while he was ahead. He'd wagered four seeds and won a hazelnut, which was worth a lot more than four seeds. It'd be best if he went to find his uncle now, got back to the task at hand. He hadn't come all this way to play gambling games. He'd come for a purpose. He just needed to get his piece of bark back.

"I'll give you double odds," Flynn proposed. "Triple odds on top of that. Win you five nuts for the price of one, you could."

Shane gasped.

"See that?" Flynn said. "My brother don't want me to bet so, but the night is young and so are you, Kit. Let's keep up the game! It's all good fun, right?"

The crowd leaned in, waiting for Kit's answer. The busy moles had stopped being busy and crowded in behind Kit to see the Blacktail brothers work. A stoat in a gray trench coat leaned over Kit's shoulder, while a whole flock of pigeons peered down on him from the dark wire above. The mangy dog outside of Larkanon's opened one eye to watch, and from the door, the skunk popped out his head at the entertainment.

"Blacktail brothers found an easy mark, eh?" he shouted. "Watch out, kid. They'll take you for that jacket and all else!"

"Do it, kiddo," the stoat in the coat urged Kit, nudging his attention back to the game. "You'll be rich by sunrise!"

"Raccoons to Riches!" called a voice from above, a finch Kit's age, fluttering over the game with a visor on his head that said NEWS. Two more young finches joined him, shouting out their own versions of the headline.

"Blacktails' Bad Luck Brings Fortune!"

"Nuts to the Newcomer!"

A chorus of voices pressured him: *"Do it!" "You'll be famous!" "Come on!" "You got 'em!"*

Kit smirked, thinking how swell it would be to show up at his uncle's place a rich raccoon. In Ankle Snap Alley, it seemed, anything was possible.

"Okay," said Kit. "I'll make that bet."

Kit would, of course, come to wish he hadn't.

Chapter Six

SURE BETS

AS soon as Kit agreed to play again, Flynn slid the hazelnut under the walnut shell again and passed a smile back to his brother. The ballyhoo began, but this time, Kit found it a lot harder to follow; Shane's paws and Flynn's tongue moved much faster.

> *Hither and thither and thither and yon,*
> *you look, you see, but where's it gone?*
> *It's time to point and pick your spot;*
> *if the nut is there, you win, why not?*

Shane stopped singing, and Kit heard the tiny sound again, the nut knocking the edge of the shell. The crowd leaned in around him, waiting with bated breath. He pointed.

"You're sure again, eh?" asked Flynn.

Kit nodded.

"Certain?"

"I'm certain," he said, suddenly wondering if Flynn was trying to get him to change his mind.

"I think you've got doubts," pressed Flynn.

"I don't," said Kit. He found the bigger raccoon's friendly smile not so friendly all of a sudden. "I'm sure."

Shane scratched behind his ears. Rather than turn over the shell, he spoke to his brother. "I don't think young Kit's very sure. He wants to change his mind."

"I don't!" Kit objected. "I am sure! That's the spot! The nut's under that shell there."

"Well, if you're so sure, let's up the bet," suggested Flynn. "All our nuts to all your seeds."

"What?" Kit felt his stomach sink. "No . . . I can't bet all my seeds . . ."

"Told you he wasn't sure," said Shane. "Kit's not the player we thought he was. Just a bit of baby fur in a shiny coat."

"I am not," Kit shouted. "I'll take that bet. You'll see!"

"The bet is made," Flynn announced for the whole crowd to hear. "Young Kit's a player after all!"

The crowd cheered again, because they loved nothing more than a high-stakes wager. If Kit won, he really would be rich. If he lost . . . well, it was too terrible to think about.

Without another word, Shane smirked, pushed the other two shells aside, and told Kit to flip over his choice.

Kit reached out, lifted the shell, and saw . . . nothing. There was no nut.

"Loser! Loser! Wrong Nut Chooser!" one of the young news finches shouted.

"Oh, come off it, Weebly." Another news finch rolled her eyes. "This ain't news. Just another sucker made a bad bet. Happens every day."

The news finches flew off to find more interesting happenings in the alley, leaving Kit dejected before the gaming table.

"But . . . I was sure of it," Kit said.

"Never be sure of anything here in Ankle Snap, young Kit," Flynn told him. "A game of chance is the least sure thing of all. Now, that's all your seeds if you please."

"I . . . I . . . ," Kit stammered.

"Or we could extend you a loan," Flynn suggested. "A line of credit to borrow. You could win and pay us back with your winnings, no harm done."

"Do it, kiddo," the stoat in the coat repeated, as if it was a line he'd memorized from a play. "You'll get 'em this time."

Kit noticed a wink pass from Flynn to the tall stoat, like they were working together. The stoat even pressed Kit forward, closer to the betting table.

The crowd around Kit urged him on, urged him to borrow from the Blacktail brothers, to play again, to double his bet with seeds he didn't have. He looked over his shoulder for another raccoon face—an uncle he'd never met, a friend of any kind—but all the faces he saw were of other animals from other families. They didn't care what happened to him, just that they were amused. Why had his mother sent him here? Why did she think he'd be safer in this place than hiding out in the forests under the Big Sky? He couldn't get out of the crowd of creatures all around. There were too many of them, not enough space, not enough sky. He felt closed in, trapped!

"Pay up or play up, young Kit." Flynn Blacktail smiled. "You've got to play to stay. Or pay what you owe and then you can go."

"I . . . I . . ." Kit reached for the seed bag in his pocket, all the money he had in the world. He had no choice. He had to turn it over. He'd lost. But in his pocket, he felt no seed pouch. All his seeds and nuts . . . all his savings were gone. Even worse, the stone was gone too . . . the Footprint of Azban! "My pouch!" he cried. "It's . . . it's . . . gone!"

Suddenly, Flynn's smile vanished. His lip raised to show his teeth, and a sharp growl slid like a knife from his snout. The crowd eased back, their senses attuned to danger.

"You said you had seeds to bet," Flynn growled. "You wouldn't be trying to cheat your cousins, now, would you, Kit?"

As Flynn spoke, Shane moved around the table, front claws up. He stood on his back paws quite a height taller than little Kit.

"We don't like moochers here," said Shane. "A bet's a bet, from howl to snap, and there's no outs from a bet made fair."

"He's right, you know," the stoat agreed.

"A bet's a bet," a mole in the crowd muttered. "Howl to snap."

"Howl to—?" Kit didn't know what they were saying. He rummaged through his pockets. He couldn't find his seed pouch anywhere. He'd been robbed; he was sure of it.

"You shouldn't play if you don't have the seeds," a squirrel in a torn bowler hat added unhelpfully.

"You owe us," said Flynn, coming around the other side of the table. "Pay up!"

"But I don't have anything to pay you with . . . ," Kit pleaded, trying to back away from the Blacktail brothers, but finding the crowd had blocked him. "My pouch was stolen, I swear it was. I have to find it!"

Through a gap in the crowd he saw a flash of white, an albino rat scurrying away down the winding alley, clutching Kit's seed pouch in her front paw.

"There," he shouted, pointing. "That rat! That rat stole my seeds!"

As all heads turned to see the rat, Kit shoved through, crawling between their legs, hopping between them and knocking them aside, running full speed after the white rat that had robbed him.

"You get back here, young Kit," Flynn Blacktail shouted after him. "You owe us. Nobody robs the Rabid Rascals!"

"Stop!" Kit called after the rat, who leaped over the dog named Rocks and dove into a wide hole in the ground next to Larkanon's.

"Watch it!" grumbled Rocks, still not bothering to move.

Kit had no choice but to swallow his fear and jump over the dog himself. He didn't even think about the angry crowd he'd left behind him, or the piece of bark on which his mother had scrawled his uncle's address in the hope Kit could find him.

He had to chase down the thieving rat and get his

pouch back. It wasn't just about his seeds. His mother had said that old stone with the Footprint of Azban on it could prevent a war. She had died protecting it. If Kit let some albino rat steal it, his parents had died for nothing.

He was not going to let that happen.

Chapter Seven

TRAPPED RAT

KIT dove into the dark hole, squeezing his body into the narrow tunnel. Though the opening was small, he popped out into a vast underground cavern. He rolled across a smooth floor, before knocking into a pile of crumbling bricks. He snatched his hat from the ground, beat the dust and dirt from it, and put it back on his head, low over his eyes while he searched the darkness for the sneaky white rat.

Creatures of all types had set up their apartments in the cavern's nooks and crannies. Two old squirrels crouched beneath an oil lamp playing cards, while a third slept under a raggedy blanket of weeds. Across from them a red fox mom was curled up with her pups, their tiny red heads poking from beneath her tail. There were other squirrels watching from high holes, guarding their nuts against intruders. In small open-front shops, possums and moles argued over the price of scraps of cloth or bits of food. There was even—Kit shuddered at the sight—a shop where a pock-faced frog in a fur-trimmed coat sold artificial claws, razor sharp, made of discarded metal scavenged from above.

"Hey, you!" the frog called out from his shop door. "Swell jacket you got on there."

Kit ignored him.

The rat was nowhere to be seen. Kit didn't dare ask anyone he saw for help. He'd learned fast what most folks down there learned young, the first rule of Ankle Snap Alley: Don't trust anybody, not even your own kind.

"I said you there! Stripy tail!" the frog called out again. "You're not from around here, are you?"

Kit kept ignoring him.

"You'll need some defense more than tooth and claw, I think," the frog said.

Kit didn't like this frog's banter and wanted to be left alone to find the rat. He figured there was one sure way to get rid of a pesky shopkeep. "I don't have any money," he said.

That was enough for the frog, who flicked his tongue

once, turned around, and hopped back into his store to wait for a better customer to come along.

"Psst." A whisper turned his head. He looked around and saw nothing. "Psst," he heard again.

Kit looked down and saw a tiny gray church mouse, wearing white robes and holding the pamphlets just like all the other church mice he'd seen. "You there," the church mouse said. "You lost?"

"I'm not lost," Kit said.

"No shame in being lost," the mouse replied. "We all get lost sometimes."

The mouse held out a pamphlet, which Kit took from him, just to be polite. On the cover was a picture of a room in a house, where two creatures sat at a table across from each other. One was a raccoon in a long and glorious coat covered with colorful feathers and cloth and beads. The other was a dog in a neat collar and a bloodred waistcoat. On the table in front of them sat a large bone, the bone of a creature much larger than either of the animals seated at the table. It was covered with tiny markings, and standing beside it was a mouse, dressed in robes just like the robes of the church mouse in front of Kit. The mouse in the drawing held a mouse-sized writing quill, and he had a mouse-sized tub of ink beside him. At the same window to the room, all kinds of creatures—furred and feathered, Flealess and Wild alike—peered in.

When Kit opened the small pamphlet, he saw the same picture, but this time the raccoon and the dog were holding their paws up in the A sign, the raccoon's sign of mutual respect, smiling, while the mouse beamed proudly at the bone in front of him, signed with the paw print of each animal. Outside the window, it looked as if a great party had erupted. Cats danced with dogs, foxes danced with hens, mice and rats and birds all danced together, with mugs of cheese ale for all.

"Do you believe the Bone is real?" the mouse asked.

"Uh." Kit had no idea what the Bone was supposed to be. He was about to ask, but the mouse talked over him without listening, as church mice so often did.

"We mice know the truth," the little mouse said. "We were the scribes at the signing. Seven hundred and seven seasons ago, we saw when the promise of peace was made. Before the betrayal of Brutus. We mice carry the truth to all mousekind."

"I'm not a mouse." Kit tried to give him the pamphlet back, but the mouse didn't take it.

"We are all mice in the eyes of history," the mouse said. "We are all of one claw if you scratch back far enough. *This* is why history must be remembered! *This* is what the mice believe. Only history will show us the way to the future!"

"Okay. Right. Um . . . I gotta go." Kit scurried on, away

from the strange mouse and his strange pronouncements.

"Son of Azban!" the mouse called. "You must know the Bone is real! Only the Bone will bring us peace!"

Kit got as far from the crazy mouse as he could. Everyone talked so strangely in this place. Everyone in Ankle Snap Alley, Kit feared, was insane. He wondered if his uncle would be too; if he ever found him.

Suddenly, a loud snap echoed through the cavern. It was followed by a piercing shriek.

"Ow! Ow! Help! I'm caught up! Help!"

"What's that?" one of the old squirrels mumbled without glancing up from his hand of cards.

"Sounds like a rat in a trap," the other answered.

"Too bad," the first replied.

"That's the way it goes, eh?" The other sighed. "From howl to snap."

"Howl to snap," concurred the first.

Neither of them moved, even as the shouting continued.

"Help! Ouch! Someone help!"

The mother fox didn't look up from her young, nor did the frog shopkeeper come out to see the cause of all the shouting. Nobody paid any attention at all to the poor creature in need. Kit's ears perked in the direction of the noise, and he followed the sounds around a bend in the wall, which led to another cavern and another tunnel, leading out again toward the light.

His mother had always taught him that the only thing worse than a liar and a cheat was a fella that heard another in need and did nothing at all to help. He wished she were here to help *him*. *He* was in need after all. Lost and robbed and on his own in a place filled with liars and cheats and lunatics.

But his troubles were no excuse.

He made his way carefully, following his ears until he found a small chamber to the left of yet another tunnel entrance. There was an abandoned shop with a faded sign that read:

GRUMPKIN'S PAW & PAWN
WE BUY & SELL.

MANAGER HAS NO KEY TO
SEED & NUT SAFE.

It looked like the place had been torn apart, completely trashed by something big and angry. The counter was tipped over and broken. All the shelves were knocked to the floor. Even the sign had a big claw mark all across it. It took Kit a moment to recognize the claw marks as words:

CLOSED BY THE FLEALESS

On the floor, behind the broken counter, Kit saw the base of a trap, a big metal contraption with a flat pressure plate and spring that snapped a bar shut when someone stepped on it.

"Help! Help!" the creature in the trap cried out.

Kit came around the counter and saw that the trap had snapped shut on the tail of the white rat, who was still holding Kit's seed pouch and crying out in pain. The rat was young, about his age, and she had on an oily brown vest with some kind of insignia on it. The insignia was so threadbare and faded that it blended into the vest almost completely. The vest itself looked like it had never been clean.

"Ouch! This really hurts! Somebody help!" the rat shouted as she squirmed in the trap.

When she saw Kit, she stopped howling and looked up at him, her tone changing instantly. She stopped shouting.

"Oh, good, it's you," she said. "Get me out of this thing. It smarts like you wouldn't believe."

Chapter Eight

HOWL TO SNAP

YOU picked my pocket!" Kit yelled at the trapped rat. "You stole all my money!"

"It was for your own good," she said. She tried to wiggle a little, but Kit saw her wince in pain. She tried to hide the grimace on her face, but she was hurting.

"Hold on." Kit sighed. "Stop wiggling."

He bent down beside the spring on the trap and studied it. The black mask of fur around his eyes crinkled as he thought. He looked it over for weak spots and then, using both his hands, he bent back one piece and unwound another part. While he did that, he stretched out one foot and used his claw to pick up a bit of dirt. He stuffed the dirt into the works of the spring, which pushed the coils apart, just enough to let the rat slide her tail out.

In a flash, she was free and standing back on her rear legs, eyeing Kit warily.

"Why'd you go and do that?" she demanded.

"Do what?" he asked.

"Get me out of that trap so quick?"

"You said you needed help." Kit shrugged. "So I helped."

"But you didn't get your pouch back first." She held up Kit's seed pouch. "You had me caught but good, and you let me go before getting what you was after."

"So?" said Kit. "I still want my pouch back. You stole it."

"I know I stole it, tick-brain!" The rat shook her head. "Point was you could've gotten it back from me while I was stuck!"

"That wouldn't have been right," Kit told her. "Just 'cause you're a two-bit crook and a cheat doesn't mean I have to be."

The rat sighed and shook her head. "You won't last long here in Ankle Snap with that attitude." She weighed the pouch in her hand. "Heavy. What you got in here?"

"That's my own business," said Kit.

"Seems to me that your business is in the palm of my paw." She tossed the little bag up and down. Kit imagined the Footprint of Azban jostling inside, cracking. His face tightened. "Oh, lighten up, big guy. You'll give your fleas a heart attack."

She tossed him the bag and rolled her eyes, watching as he stuffed it into the front pocket of his jacket. "Put it inside your jacket," she said. "Harder to snatch."

"That's where it was," he said.

"Harder for anyone but *me* to snatch," she clarified.

Kit scowled, but did like she suggested.

"I'm no crook, by the way," the rat called out. "My name's Eeni. And you are?"

"I'm Kit." He stopped and turned back around to face her. "And where I come from, if you pick somebody's pocket, that makes you a crook."

"I was always gonna give it back to you. I told you I stole it for your own good."

"My own good? How's that?"

"You had to get away from them Blacktail brothers. Bad news they are. Getting you to chase me seemed the best way. You were about a breath and a half away from getting rabbit-rolled."

"Rabbit-rolled?" Kit wondered.

"Nailed to the wall by your ears by one brother while the other robs you blind. If you struggle, the nails stretch your ears out like a rabbit's."

"That's awful. They seemed so nice."

"Folks in Ankle Snap Alley always *seem* nice," she

said. "But half of them are liars and half of them are pick-pockets and the last half of them's both."

"Three halves? That doesn't add up honest."

"Ankle Snap Alley's the kind of place where things don't add up honest. They never have."

Kit frowned.

"So where'd you learn to open traps like that?" Eeni asked him.

He shrugged. "Back home."

"You from the Big Sky?" Eeni asked.

"Yeah," said Kit.

"Why'd you leave swell turf like that for here?" Eeni wondered. "Slivered Sky and the gritty old Ankle Snap."

"I've come to find my uncle," said Kit.

"Find him? He lost?"

"I don't know. I've never met him. He's my mother's brother. My ma gave me his address on a piece of bark, and told me to find him . . . but . . ."

"But you lost that piece of bark to the Blacktail brothers?"

Kit nodded.

"You don't remember what she wrote?"

Kit shook his head. He felt tears pressing on the back of his eyes.

"Well, don't worry about that," said Eeni. "You know

this uncle's name? We can't very well go asking around for any old uncle."

"His name's Rik," he said.

"Just Rik? That ain't much to go on. Maybe it's best you head back home."

"I can't do that," Kit said firmly. "You gonna help me?"

"You helped me when you didn't have to," said Eeni. "And a rat always returns a favor, so, yeah, I'll help you. Howl to snap."

"'Howl to snap'? What is that?" asked Kit. "I heard some other folks saying it."

"Howl to snap?" The rat brought her tail around and sucked on the tip where it was bruised. She leaned back against the wall. Rats felt best when they were leaning against walls. "It's just a thing we say around here. You know, you're born under this sky howling, and most often as not, you go out with the snap of a trap. Same's true for everyone. But what you do between that howl and that snap, well, that's what matters. Every lie you tell or kindness you create. The stuff you do from howl to snap makes you who you are. Get it?"

"I get it," said Kit. "Thanks."

She shrugged. "Don't let it ever be said I'm not a rat who keeps her word."

"Just one who picks pockets." Kit smirked.

"When necessary. So, this uncle of yours? Anything else you know about him? How's he make his nuts? He a seed swiper? Paper tickler? Plain old robbing raccoon?"

"No!" said Kit. "He's not a criminal at all! My uncle's like my parents. He's a historian."

"*An* historian," Eeni corrected him. "And that's even worse. History's a dangerous business around these parts." She pointed up at the scratched sign to the old Paw & Pawn. "The hedgehog who ran this place had an interest in history. He sold all kinds of historical artifacts to all kinds of folks and then he refused to pay the Rabid Rascals for protection. Said history gave him a right to be here and he wasn't gonna pay 'em for a right that was his by birth. Without the Rascals protecting him, the Flealess shut him down, kidnapped his woodpecker assistant too. Better your uncle were a paper tickler than an historian. They live longer."

"What is a paper tickler?"

"Don't you learn anything out in the Big Sky? Paper tickler's a card cheat. They tickle the paper cards to make 'em jump."

"Oh . . . right." Kit thought about his uncle. If he was also in danger, then Kit had better find him fast. He couldn't stand here in an abandoned shop learning new lingo all night. "So, where do we look for him?"

"Normally, I'd say we just ask the Blacktail brothers, because they don't miss a trick around here, but we can't go back to them. My guess is they're still snarling mad and best avoided."

"Why should they be mad? *They're* the ones who cheated *me*."

"But *you're* the one who let himself get cheated," Eeni said. "Better be more careful in the future."

"Isn't anybody down here honest?" Kit wondered.

"Sure." Eeni patted Kit on the back. "You are!"

Kit frowned.

"Listen, Kit," she told him. "Honest fellas around here learn quick to keep quiet. Many an honest fella has disappeared into the sewers for talking too much. Everybody who comes here's got a secret. They're either running from someplace or running to someplace or stuck right in this alley with no place else to go. This is home for folks who ain't got a home anyplace else. The Flealess in those buildings all around, they want to get rid of all of us and take the alley for themselves. They terrorize us every chance they get. So the Rabid Rascals help out . . . for a price. Most of them are runaway house pets themselves, and the ones that ain't—the Blacktail brothers and the like—well, they're clever and mean and dangerous too. Folks pay the Rascals for protection, and the Rascals keep the Flealess away. Folks who don't pay, or who make the Rascals mad, well . . ." She gestured at the torn-up shop around them. "Bad things happen to 'em."

"Why are you telling me all this?"

Eeni picked at the frayed seal on her vest. "Just to tell you that folks here ain't all liars; they're just . . . circumspect."

"Circum-what?"

"Spect. Circumspect," Eeni told him. "Means that they don't take risks when they don't have to."

"So you aren't like other folks down here, then?" said Kit. "Taking a risk to help me out. You aren't so *circumspect* at all."

"Me?" Eeni shrugged. "I'm just a sucker for an honest fella. Howl to snap."

"Howl to snap," Kit repeated, but he felt, of a sudden, circumspect himself, even as he followed Eeni up into the moonlight. "If we can't ask the Blacktail brothers about Uncle Rik, who are we going to ask?"

Eeni called back over her shoulder as she made her way from the small shop. "Why, we're going to ask the Brood, of course!"

Chapter Nine

THE BROOD

KIT and Eeni popped from beneath a shed just down the narrow lane from where the Black-tail brothers were still at their work, luring in whatever gapers they could find. Their voices carried through the night.

Quick of eye and quick of paw,
bet some seeds and win 'em all . . .

Kit glanced nervously in their direction, but Eeni beckoned him with her little hand. "Don't mind about them for now." She led Kit behind the chicken coop, where a brood of chickens were clucking their nightly gossip.

"I hear that church mouse minister takes a thimbleful of cheese ale daily," one of the chickens clucked.

"I hear it's more like two thimbles!" another squawked.

The largest of all the chickens, a big lady sitting on a hearty number of eggs, sang a little tune to the others. *"A thimble of ale, be it cheddar or Swiss, has lured many a mouse down to Gayle's Abyss."* The others clucked wildly as the big lady continued. *"A rooster I knew who took his ale blue. The cheese was quite stinky, his breath was quite too."*

"Another! Another!" the other chickens cried.

"What are we doing here?" Kit wondered.

Eeni rolled her eyes. "Everyone knows that if you want to know something, you ask the birds. You just got to be careful, because birds love to gossip, and they don't mind so much if what they say is true or not. Come on."

As they approached, the big hen hushed her friends and peered down her spectacles at Eeni and Kit.

"Now, now, young'uns," she called out. "What brings you to my fine roost on a night such as this?"

"We're looking for someone, Miss Costlecrunk," Eeni replied.

"Oh, crack my shell, it's 'Miss' now is it?!" The big chicken laughed. "I haven't been Miss Costlecrunk since before the Cat Wars. It's 'Missus' to you, dear."

"Yes, Missus," said Eeni.

"Now who's your friend?" Her head turned to the side,

her neck bobbing back and forth with a jiggle. The side eye took in Kit from paw to claw. "Handsome lad."

Kit felt a blush on his snout.

"Oh! Oh," Mrs. Costlecrunk cried. "I'd no notion a raccoon could blush so!"

"Must be from the Big Sky," another chicken chimed in. "Won't find a Blacktail brother blushing."

"A blush is a sign of manners, I'd say," Mrs. Costlecrunk replied. "We could use more blushing and less brazenness here in the Ankle Snap." She addressed Kit directly. "You are most welcome here—?"

"Kit," he told her.

"Kit. Most welcome." A chorus of clucks echoed her. "But do watch yourself. This is no place to share your blushes with the moonlight. Add some swagger to your step, and you'll be all right."

"I'll try to . . . uh . . . swagger," said Kit.

"We're looking for his uncle," Eeni explained. "Goes by the name Rik." Eeni dropped her voice to a whisper. *"He's an historian."*

"Oh, a nephew of Rik's, is it?" Mrs. Costlecrunk eyed Kit again, more circumspect this time. "Well." The big hen sighed. "In that case . . ."

She held out a foot, stretching her leg down from her perch to hang in front of Kit's face. He cocked his head at the taloned bird foot. She snapped her chicken toes and held her foot flat right in front of him. Kit didn't know what to do, so he slapped her claw with his black paw, trying to be friendly.

"What are you doing?!" Eeni marveled.

"I . . . uh . . . was giving her five?"

Eeni shook her head and whispered in his ear, "She wants a bribe."

"What happened to helping people out who need help?" he whispered back.

"You're in Ankle Snap Alley," she said. "No one does anything for free."

Kit considered his options, then reached into his pocket and pulled a few seeds from his pouch without letting anyone see the stone inside. He dropped the seeds into Mrs. Costlecrunk's open foot. She clenched her toes around the seeds and withdrew them underneath her body once more, ruffling her feathers and preening a moment to regain her composure after the surprising and unwelcome "low five" from the young raccoon.

"Well," she said at last. "You can find your uncle Rik— Riky Two Rings they call him—at the base of the Gnarly Oak Apartments . . . but I don't think you should."

"Why not?" Kit asked. "I mean, Why not, Mrs. Costlecrunk, ma'am?"

The hen clucked. "He doesn't take well to visitors. Just two nights ago he chased off a flock of young news finches looking for a story on the woodpecker, and everyone knows he's littered his garden with traps. A church mouse nearly lost his tail trying to shove a pamphlet in the door just this evening."

"He'll want to see me," said Kit.

"Oh, I've no doubt." Mrs. Costlecrunk smirked. "But mind your tail all the same, boy. I'd hate to see a redder blush flood that fine fur of yours."

"Thank you for your help, ladies." Eeni curtsied to the hens. Kit wasn't sure of the right thing to do, so he curtsied too, which brought out a whole new round of laughter from the brood. Kit tried not to share his blushing with the moonlight again, but he felt his snout redden anyway.

"Now listen here, Kit." The big hen adjusted her glasses on her beak. "Mind your step in the alley, lad. Not all traps are made of metal. Sometimes words can be the most dangerous snares of all."

"Uh . . . okay . . . I'll remember that." Kit wasn't sure he had any idea what the chicken was on about. Everyone in Ankle Snap Alley had such a funny way of talking. Words were another game to play, like shells-and-nuts, and wherever you thought the meaning was hid, they'd hid it somewhere else altogether. You couldn't win, but you had to play. Kit wondered if he'd ever learn to talk like them, and he wondered if this place would ever feel like home.

Chapter Ten

RIKY TWO RINGS

WHATEVER you're selling, I'm not buying," a deep voice boomed through the wooden door at the base of the Gnarly Oak Apartments. "Go away."

Uncle Rik's apartment was tucked among the tangled roots of a massive oak tree that filled the north end of Ankle Snap Alley. The tree's canopy was taller than the People's buildings, stretching from rooftop to rooftop. The upper branches were filled with birds' nests and squirrel holes and the mixed and matched apartments of a hundred other creatures. Their laundry rustled in the breeze between the leaves, drying slowly in the moonlight. The tree's base was a warren of cramped holes where rat, woodpecker, squirrel, and raccoon rented their turf from the birds above, payment in full at the start of each season.

There was trash strewn all around the base of the tree, garbage that People had tossed into the alley without a thought for the furred and feathered citizens living there. A giant truck tire rested in the dirt beside the door to Uncle Rik's apartment.

Uncle Rik's door was a round barrel top wedged into an arched root that rose up taller than Kit could stand. There was a sliding metal bar that opened just wide enough for the raccoon inside to peer out. His asphalt-black eyes raked over Kit and Eeni.

"I said go away!" he shouted through the door.

"But, Uncle Rik," Kit pleaded, "it's your nephew, Kit! Your sister's son. I'm not selling anything. I'm family."

"I've got no family," Uncle Rik snapped, then he slid the metal bar shut with a thud.

"He doesn't want to see you, I guess," Eeni said sadly.

Kit sucked in air through his pointy teeth. He had come a long way from the big skies of home. He'd nearly been robbed and rabbit-rolled by hoodlums. He'd met sketchy frogs and gossiping chickens and a strange mouse squeaking at him about a bone that could bring peace.

He was not going to be turned away by his own uncle.

Kit clenched his little black fists and pounded on the door until the slot opened again.

"You do *too* have a family," Kit shouted. "*I'm* your family, and I've come all this way to find you, and I'm not going away until you let me in."

"Go home, Kit," the deep voice boomed. "Go back to your mom and dad under the Big Sky. The city is no place for the likes of you."

"I can't go home," Kit said, and now he felt the pressure of tears, his eyes like a beaver dam about to burst. "My home got destroyed. My mom and dad are dead."

Eeni froze beside him, shocked. The eyes behind the slit of door widened and then dropped. A sad sigh slid through the crack. The door creaked as it swung open.

"Dead?" Uncle Rik, a gray-and-black raccoon, wearing a tattered plaid robe, stood upright in the doorway. He had a stubby snout, long whiskers, and big black-cherry eyes, suddenly filled with sad surprise. At his feet lay a book he must have dropped. Its cover was splayed open like the wings of a bat.

**A History of the Turf Wars, Volume Seven
By Rev. H. Mus Musculus III**

His uncle paid the fallen book no attention. "Both of them?"

Kit nodded. Now that he'd said the words out loud for the first time, it felt real, too real. He had pressed the thoughts to the back of his mind for the entire journey, but now he couldn't keep the memories away any longer. They swarmed him like fleas. They bit.

His parents were dead.

He burst into tears. The black fur around his eyes glistened as if it were studded with diamonds. The diamonds fell into the dirt, splattered, and his uncle, glancing up and down the alley, beckoned Kit and Eeni quickly inside.

"Watch the tire," he said as they slipped past it. "Filled with traps."

When they were inside, Uncle Rik triple-locked the door behind them. They came into a messy living room with a threadbare couch patched with the same fabric as Uncle Rik's robe. There were notes and books covering the broken chairs, strange artifacts and packs of mismatched playing cards on the shelves, several lamps burning on a low table, and countless half-empty mugs of bitter black acorn brew.

Uncle Rik moved some papers and bits of bark off a chair and helped Kit to sit down. He didn't pay any attention to Eeni, but she didn't mind. She wasn't paying any attention to herself either. She was staring at Kit, who had been carrying around his tragedy without a word all these hours.

"My sister?" Uncle Rik's voice creaked. His face sagged like a plastic bag caught in the branches of a tree. "And your dad?"

"Uh-huh." Kit sniffled. "They sent me here . . . my ma . . . she said you could help . . . there's no one else . . ."

"What happened?" Uncle Rik asked. "I mean . . . uh . . . if you want to talk about it."

Kit tried to pull himself together.

"I'll get you some . . . uh . . ." Uncle Rik didn't know what to offer. "I only have acorn brew or cheese ale?"

"We're too young for cheese ale," Eeni told him.

"Right . . . acorn brew, then."

"We're too young for that too," she said.

"I'll bring some water." He scurried from the room, half dazed.

"I'm so sorry, Kit," Eeni said when they were alone. "I had no idea . . ."

Kit shook his head. "I didn't want to tell you. I didn't want to say it. I thought if I didn't say it out loud, it wouldn't be real. Like it was all a dream, this house, this alley. Even you."

"I'm not a dream, Kit," she said. "I'm your friend now, howl to snap."

Kit wiped his nose with his paw. "Howl to snap."

"Here's some water." Uncle Rik handed him a big cup of water, so big he had to hold it with both hands. It was pink and People-made. Kit had never drunk from a People's cup before, but he lifted it to his mouth and gulped. He hadn't even realized how thirsty he was.

While he drank, Eeni stood by his side, and his uncle dropped himself down onto the couch, sweeping his bathrobe out underneath him. He looked at Kit, his face folded in a frown. "Do you want to talk about it?" he asked.

Kit nodded. He didn't really want to talk about it, but he knew that Uncle Rik had lost his sister, and he had a right to know what had happened. He needed to know *what* had happened, if Kit was ever going to understand *why* it had happened.

Kit had learned something during his few hours in Ankle Snap Alley. Nobody did anything for free in this place. Everything cost something, and the price of Kit finding answers would be this: He would have to tell the story of what happened that day, he would have to say it out loud, and by saying it, he knew he would have to live it again in his mind.

Sometimes telling a story hurt worse than living it, but sometimes telling the stories that hurt the most was the only way to survive.

"I couldn't save them," Kit began. "I tried, but I couldn't save them."

Chapter Eleven

A DEBT IS DUE

THE dogs pounced on her because that six-clawed cat made them. And that's why I came here." Kit finished his story, leaving out nothing. The fur on his cheeks was damp, and he wiped his eyes with his tail.

Eeni and Uncle Rik looked at him quietly, pity scratched across both their faces. But Kit didn't want pity. He wanted to keep his promise to his mother, to grow up brave and quick of paw and to help Uncle Rik finish the work his parents had begun, just like she had told him to.

Uncle Rik appeared to understand. "Did you bring the Footprint?" he asked.

Kit pulled out his seed pouch and removed the stone with the small footprint on it. He passed it to Uncle Rik, whose eyes lit with awe.

"Well, shave my tail, they really found it!" Uncle Rik exclaimed. "A real Footprint of Azban."

"Like, Azban, the First Raccoon?" Eeni asked, leaning forward to sniff at the stone with her tiny pink nose.

Uncle Rik nodded.

"You mean . . . when I stole the pouch . . . I stole . . . ?" Her whiskers sagged as her jaw hung open.

Kit nodded at her. "See why I chased you down?"

"That must be worth a fortune," Eeni said. "There are collectors who'd pay anything you asked for a real footprint of one of the First Animals."

"Oh, certainly there are," said Uncle Rik.

"Is that why they killed my parents? Just to get rich?" Kit was disgusted.

"Oh no," said Uncle Rik. "The dogs who attacked your home did not want the footprint to sell it. They wanted the footprint to destroy it."

"Well, that makes as much sense as a platypus in a parachute." Eeni shook her head. "Who'd go destroying something they could turn a profit on? Wouldn't catch folk from Ankle Snap Alley throwing away an easy score."

"I fear the ones who did this are terribly close to Ankle

Snap Alley," said Uncle Rik. "In fact, Ankle Snap Alley is at the center of this entirely. Kit, do you know what this footprint means?"

He remembered his mother saying this little stone could help stop a war, but he couldn't imagine how.

"It's a clue!" Uncle Rik exclaimed. "This is the clue your parents had been searching for their whole lives. This is the proof that Azban was real. And that Azban was here, long ago. This could lead us right to the Bone of Contention."

"I heard a mouse talking about the Bone of Contention," Kit said. "He tried to give me a pamphlet."

"That's mice for you," Eeni grumbled. "Always trying make everybody read all the time. As if reading ever helped anybody." She crossed her arms and harrumphed.

Kit cocked his head at Eeni, wondering what she had against reading, but right now, he didn't want to get distracted. Right now, he wanted to know what the Bone of Contention was and why his mother believed it could stop a war. Why his parents had to die for it.

"The Bone is an ancient contract," his uncle began, "between Azban and Brutus, the Duke of Dogs. Some say it never existed, but for those who believe in it, it gives the wild creatures all the—"

Just then, someone pounded on the front door so loud it made them jump.

"Who's that?" Kit whispered.

"Hush." Uncle Rik tensed and bared his teeth. "I'm not expecting any visitors tonight."

He slid the Footprint of Azban back into Kit's seed pouch and handed the pouch back to him, then his claws came out. He crept toward the door. Before Uncle Rik was even half the distance down the hall, the door bent, like it was being squeezed from the outside, and then burst, sending splinters of wood flying in all directions.

Kit and Eeni peeked out into the hall and saw, much to their dismay, the Blacktail brothers, Flynn and Shane, in the open doorway, and behind them, his body uncoiling, a massive python. It was the same brown-and-yellow python Kit had seen collecting payoffs from the small business owners. The python's rows of needle-sharp teeth glistened in the moonlight.

"Riky Two Ringssss," the python hissed. "Sssso good to sssseee you thissss evening."

"And there's Kit, our old friend," said Shane Blacktail with an oil-slick smile.

"*Young* friend, you mean, brother," Flynn Blacktail responded. "If Kit were older he'd know that you don't run out on a losing bet before you've paid. Not on your worst enemy and certainly not on your friends."

"We'd like to stay friends," Shane said. "And we'd like young Kit to grow old."

"We certainly would," agreed Flynn. "Can't be an old friend if you don't grow old at all."

"What do you want with my nephew?" Uncle Rik demanded.

"Were we not clear?" said Shane.

"I thought we were terribly clear," said Flynn.

"Riky Two Rings doesn't listen well," said Shane.

"Perhaps he'll listen to Basil." Flynn snapped his fingers. "Basil. Make him listen."

Basil the python slid his large body past the two raccoons, filling the hallway, and slithered face-to-face with Kit's uncle. Kit and Eeni clutched each other nervously, but Uncle Rik didn't move a muscle. He locked eyes with the snake.

"We just want what's owed us," Flynn called out from the other side of the python.

"Plus a fee for our troubles," added Shane.

"Your troubles haven't started yet," Uncle Rik warned, and his chest puffed up so his body seemed to fill the hallway, blocking the snake from slithering even one scale farther.

"Ssssuch a big talker," Basil said. "Makessss me wanna sssssqueeze the talk right out of him."

"If my nephew has a debt, I'll pay it," said Uncle Rik. "But only if it's fairly owed. We both know that the Black-tail brothers never won a bet fair in their lives."

"Slander!" Flynn Blacktail cried out.

"Lies!" Shane echoed him.

"Slander *and* lies!" Flynn concurred. He held a paw up to the sky and spoke in a singsongy voice. "I swear before Azban himself that our games are twice as honest as any under the Slivered Sky."

"Twice of none is still none," said Uncle Rik.

"We didn't invent math," Shane replied. "Kit lost his bet and ran out on paying. That's a fact more true than any multiplication table."

"I didn't lose," Kit called out. "They cheated. I knew where the nut was, but they must've moved it with sleight of paw."

"Ssssoundsssss like your nephew doessssn't want to pay," Basil said. His body coiled forward underneath him. He reared himself back to strike. "Sssssoundsssss like ssssomeone'ssss got to pay or ssssomeone'ssss got to get hurt—"

"You leave them alone!" Eeni shouted. "We all know the Blacktail brothers cheated."

The snake grinned at her. "Yum," he said. "A ssssnack! Doessss anyone know if white ratssss are ssssaltier than gray onessss?"

"If your bets are so fair," Uncle Rik proposed, "why not make one more?"

"Another bet?" Shane said.

"For what stakes?" Flynn said.

"Forgive what my nephew owes," Uncle Rik said.

"And if you lose this bet?" asked Shane.

"I'll pay double," said Uncle Rik.

"Tssss, tssss, tssss," Basil broke out into a loud, sibilant snake laugh. He laughed so hard all his coils shook and his head hit the ceiling, showering the hall with dust and dirt. "You? Pay double? You owe ussss more than you've got already."

"I'm good for it," said Uncle Rik, but Kit noticed his uncle's snout blushing in the same way Kit's did. A family trait. It made the whole family bad at bluffing. Judging by the mess his house was in even before the snake busted down the door, Uncle Rik didn't have a lot of seeds or nuts to lose in a bet.

"You ssssaid you were 'good for it' at the cockroach fightssss lasssst week," said Basil. "And at the ssssparrow racccccessss before that. You're in deep to the bossss."

"I . . . er . . ." Uncle Rik looked at his feet, embarrassed to be called out in front of his nephew. Uncle Rik was a gambler, and not one gifted with either skill or luck.

"We've learned better than to make bets with a historian," said Flynn.

"An historian," said Eeni.

"What?" said Flynn.

"An historian," Eeni corrected him. "It's the indefinite article preceding a vowel sound."

"What?" said Flynn.

"You said *'a' historian*," said Eeni. "But it should've been 'an' historian. I'm just saying, if you're gonna insult a fella, get your grammar right."

"You're a smart one," said Flynn.

"Too smart for a gutter rat," said Shane.

"I know what I know." Eeni folded her arms.

"Well, here's something for you to know, Eeni," said Flynn. "How long does it take a python to eat a raccoon?"

"She doesn't know," said Shane. "Basil. Show her. Eat Kit."

Chapter Twelve

RETIREMENT FUND

BASIL'S coils wrapped themselves around Kit and squeezed. The snake's mouth opened wider than Kit's whole head, and his breath smelled like rodent bones and cheese ale.

Kit would not be Basil's first meal of the day.

"Uncle Rik! Help!" Kit screamed.

Eeni punched at Basil's scaly side.

"How dare you come into my home to eat my nephew," Uncle Rik yelled, rather unhelpfully.

Kit realized if he was going to get saved, he was going

to have to save himself. He couldn't wriggle free, and he couldn't pry himself free. Although he had always been good at using his hands to get out of traps, they wouldn't help this time. He'd have to use his wits instead.

"Uncle! Please!" he pleaded in his most desperate voice. "Just give them your secret stash of seeds."

"What?" Rik looked puzzled.

"Your life savings!" Kit tried to wink at his uncle without anyone else seeing. "Your reTIREment fund?"

"My—wha—?" Uncle Rik began, then it dawned on him. "Oh . . . oh no . . . Kit, that's worth far too much."

Flynn raised an eyebrow. Shane cocked his head to the side. Even Basil slowed his squeezing.

Uncle Rik played it up now. "I'm sorry, kiddo, you're a real pal of the paw and all that, but I've only just met you. I've spent my whole life collecting my secret seed savings. I fear I'll miss them far more than I'll miss a nephew. Apologies."

"But . . . Uncle!"

"No, no, no. Sorry, Kit. Squeeze on, Basil." Uncle Rik waved his paw in the air. "Just eat my nephew quickly and then we're even."

"Wait a moment, Basil," Flynn instructed the snake. "I'd like to hear more about this retirement fund."

"I won't say a word about it." Uncle Rik crossed his arms. "Those are my seeds and nuts and scraps and scroungings, and I won't share with anyone."

"Tell me, Kit." Shane smiled. "Would you like *not* to be eaten?"

Kit couldn't talk anymore because the snake's squeezing was too tight, but he nodded.

"Do you know where your uncle keeps his secret wealth?" Flynn asked.

Kit nodded again.

"No, Kit, please don't tell them!" Uncle Rik cried out, then pretended to faint onto his sofa, which Kit thought was a bit much, but the Blacktail brothers didn't seem to notice the bad performance. They were thinking about robbing secret riches now and had no room in their raccoon brains for anything else.

Basil loosened his grip and Kit took a big breath. He wiggled himself higher up on the snake's back so he could look down on the Blacktail brothers.

"Well? Where issss the loot?" Basil demanded.

"There's a big tire outside," said Kit. "He hides it there."

"Outside?" Shane looked doubtful.

"Of course," said Kit. "That's the safest place. You hear about houses getting robbed all the time, and if he kept all his seeds here, they'd get robbed too. But you never hear about someone's tire getting robbed. No one robs a tire."

"It's true," added Eeni. "I've never heard about a tire robbery."

"You keep quiet," Flynn told her. "In fact, why don't *you* go check it out for us. That way, if it's a trick, you'll be the one who gets tricked."

Eeni nodded and moved for the door, brushing past Kit with a reassuring squeeze of his paw. The others followed her outside—except Uncle Rik, who was enjoying his role, pretending to have fainted.

The Blacktail brothers, with Kit, Basil, and Eeni, stood around the tire outside. A passing squirrel looked away from them, while two news finches pretended not to watch from a high branch. Their little heads tilted with anticipation of a good story to sing about. Windows in the Gnarly Oak Apartments slammed shut so that the eyes of young bunnies, foxes, rats, and mice wouldn't see the ugly scene about to unfold below.

Kit couldn't believe that a whole crowded neighborhood could see the trouble he was in, yet no one moved to help.

But everyone in Ankle Snap Alley knew that creatures who went around witnessing things had a way of vanishing into the sewers or slipping onto the train tracks. Better to see nothing, hear nothing, know nothing, and do nothing. Safer that way. Kit understood the word *circumspect* now for real, and he didn't like it. He was certain if he ever saw another creature in desperate straits like he was in, he wouldn't be at all circumspect. He'd help.

"Get in there!" Shane ordered Eeni.

The white rat sighed and scrambled up the side of the tire, then glanced back at Kit, who tried to warn her with his eyes to be careful. She winked, then vanished inside the tire.

"Wow!" she called out. "There's too much in here to carry!"

"Prove it!" Flynn called out.

A pouch came flying from inside the tire and landed right in front of the raccoons. It was bursting with seeds and nuts. Kit recognized it as his own seed pouch . . . Eeni had swiped it again when she'd brushed past him! How could she risk the Footprint of Azban like this?

Kit tried not to let the surprise or panic show on his face, but he needn't have worried. The Blacktail brothers weren't looking at him. They smiled at each other, and both bent down to pick up the pouch at the same time. Their foreheads knocked together.

"Ouch," barked Flynn.

"Hey," barked Shane. "I'll take this pouch, you take the next one."

"Why don't I take this little thing," said Flynn. "I'm sure there's a bigger one for you in there."

"Oh, I couldn't take the bigger one from my own brother," said Shane. "I'll take this little one, and you take the next."

"Hey," Basil interrupted them. "We ssssplit that by three. Not two. I want my share."

"Of course, of course," said Flynn. "Once we've seen what's what, we'll split it nice and evenly, three ways."

Basil's eyes narrowed to suspicious slits. Flynn's and Shane's did too. In a flash, they all sprang for the tire, none of them trusting the other not to take as much as he could for himself. They all dove in, just as Eeni hopped out and hit the ground with a smile.

SNAP! SNAP! SNAP!

Three traps snapped shut inside the tire.

"Ow!" yelled Shane.

"Ow!" yelled Flynn.

"Sssssssss!" hissed Basil.

Kit made the A sign with his paws, and Eeni returned the gesture. "Nasty traps in there," she said. "Easy to avoid if you're expecting them, though."

"Too bad those three weren't expecting them, then?" Kit replied, bending to pick up his seed pouch from the ground. Eeni handed him the stone with the footprint on it. She'd taken it out before throwing the pouch to the crooks.

"I didn't want to risk it falling into the wrong paws," she said with a smile.

"You don't miss a trick, do you?" asked Kit.

"Neither do you, huh, Kit?" said Eeni. "You're a sharp one."

"Sharp enough to cut yourself," said Uncle Rik, leaning on the doorframe of his apartment with a grin on his face and a paw resting in his pocket.

"You get us out of here, Riky Two Rings!" Shane yelled.

"You're a lousy, cheating sneak, Kit!" added Flynn.

"Ssssssss," added Basil, whose head had been clamped in a metal trap and whose body wriggled and shook the whole tire violently. The back of his body poked out from the tube, thrashing wildly.

"So, what do we do with them?" Kit asked.

Uncle Rik looked up and down the alley, and wiped his paws on his robe. "Well, I think we should clean some of the garbage out of this alley!"

Together, the three of them heaved and hefted and levered and lifted the tire up, as the snake and the twin raccoon rascals hurled all manner of curses at them.

"We'll get you for this, you hairball-hacking traitors!"

"No one treats a Rabid Rascal this way!"

"Sssssssssss!"

"Ready?" said Uncle Rik with a laugh in his voice. "A one and a two and a three!"

With that, Kit, Eeni, and Rik sent the tire rolling down the length of Ankle Snap Alley. Moles and stoats and church mice dove from its path as it picked up speed, bouncing and spinning and hurling along. Even the mangy dog in front of Larkanon's opened one eye to watch the truck tire streak past.

"Gahhhhhhhhhh!" screamed the three hoodlums trapped inside, as they smashed through the fence and flew clear over the train tracks and out of Ankle Snap Alley. A round of applause erupted from all the creatures on the street, furred and feathered alike. Even the big rooster in his barbershop clapped his wings, before returning to sweeping fur from the floor.

"Well, that's that sorted out." Uncle Rik clapped his paws as if nothing at all remarkable had happened. "Say, why don't we go over to Ansel's bakery and get a bite to eat. He makes the best trash casserole beneath the Slivered Sky. I'm buying!"

Kit smiled and licked his lips. He was starving, and trash casserole was just what he needed after the single longest night of his young life.

"And while we're there, perhaps I can tell you more about this stone you've got," Uncle Rik added in a whisper. "And how it could change everything."

As his uncle pulled the busted door into place as best he could and led Kit and Eeni back through the alley toward Possum Ansel's bakery, an orange cat watched from his favorite shadow between two buildings. Next to him, the miniature greyhound growled.

"That's the one?" the dog asked the cat.

"That's the one who got away," the cat confirmed.

Titus pawed at the dirt. "You think he has the footprint."

"I do," said the cat.

"How do you know?" the dog growled.

"A little bird told me." Sixclaw burped, and a single finch's feather fell from his mouth. "Before I ate him."

"If that clue leads him to the Bone of Contention, we'll have a problem," said the dog.

"So you want me to kill him?"

"Kill all three of them," said the dog. "Just to be sure."

"If the Bone is real, then don't the vermin have a right to Ankle Snap Alley?"

"That's why the Bone must *stay* buried," said the dog. "Their time in Ankle Snap Alley is over, and I will see these vermin evicted. No crazy deal some great-great-great-great-granddog of mine made will stop me from getting rid of them."

"Brutus was no granddog of yours," said the cat, but Titus shot him a withering glance.

Sixclaw yawned. He didn't care much who he killed or why or what history had to say about it. Dogs loved territory and would do anything to claim it, but Sixclaw, like most cats, simply enjoyed the act of killing. The young raccoon's parents were a good start, but he should've taken care of the young one himself, instead of leaving the hunting dogs to do it. There was, after all, nothing quite so satisfying to an outdoor cat as a young life cut short by his own claws.

He stretched his back and crept off into the dark, the tiny bell on his collar dinging as he disappeared.

Part III

MAKING BONES

Chapter Thirteen

KIT CASSEROLE

A sign outside of P. Ansel's Sweet & Best-Tasting Baking Company advertised the night's specials:

Daily Trash Casserole

Canned tuna and apple core with chocolate sprinkles, beef-bone-and-ant puree in an orange-and-lettuce-juice reduction sauce. Potato chip crust.

Side of fried grubs or carrot stems (vegetarian option).

Kit's stomach grumbled as his uncle held the door for him. Inside, all manner of creatures had gathered to eat, filling the tattered booths, perching on the stools along the brightly lit counter, and lining up from one end of the store to the other to ogle the pastries and treats in the overflowing cases (which were made from the windshields of People's cars).

Kit's eyes went wide at the stale-sourdough pudding, the lemon-peel honey brittle, the worm-and-bubble-gum-chew pies, and barrels and barrels of acorn candy. He'd never seen so many delicious scroungings.

"Three casseroles, Ansel," Uncle Rik called out over the crowd, and the big possum behind the counter popped his head up, his red eyes gleaming. Then he froze, completely still, with a cup of sour-cream beet sorbet in his hand. He looked like a statue of a possum serving sour-cream beet sorbet.

"Look what you've done!" shouted a squirrel perched on a stool at the end of the counter. "You've made him play possum! It'll take forever to get our food now!"

"It's not my fault," Uncle Rik objected as all the customers glared angrily at him. Possum Ansel was the most popular chef in the alley, and folks got impatient waiting for their turn to try his famous treats. "Hey, P, wake up!" Uncle Rik snapped his claws.

The possum shuddered and shook himself awake. All heads turned from Uncle Rik back to Ansel. His red eyes narrowed.

"You've got a lot of nerve coming here, Riky Two Rings," Possum Ansel hissed, flexing his claws.

A big badger popped his long nose out from the kitchen in the back. He wore an apron over a striped shirt with the sleeves rolled up to his massive elbows. The big white stripe down the center of his face was speckled with chocolate frosting. "You want me to throw him to the street, Ansel?"

"Now, listen here, Ansel, there's no need for Otis to do that," Uncle Rik spluttered. "I've got my nephew in from the Big Sky and his friend here, and we're just trying to get some dinner. I know you and I have had our disagreements in the past, but there's no need to resort to violence in front of the young'uns. Whatever I owe you, I swear I can pay soon. I'm just a little short on seeds right now, but if you'll wait—"

The badger stepped all the way from the kitchen, his body filling the door, menacing in the way only a badger in an apron can menace.

"Hi, Otis, old pal. You're looking well these days . . . ," Uncle Rik simpered.

Otis cracked his knuckles.

"Listen, Ansel, I swear I'll pay for my dinner tonight," Uncle Rik pleaded.

"Your money's no good here," Possum Ansel told Uncle Rik. In a corner booth, a skinny pigeon cooed. The tension crackled like a squirrel gnawing through a power line.

"I . . . I'm just trying to . . ." Uncle Rik was at a loss for words.

"Because whatever you want is on the house!" the possum exclaimed, throwing his paws up and bursting out in an uproarious laugh. The big badger laughed too, and all the customers cheered and clapped and barked and squawked. "You gave those Blacktail goons what for, and for that, I thank you! They shake me down once a week and never pay for their food. Any enemy of theirs is a friend of mine. Sit, please. This is your nephew? Handsome lad! And his rodent friend? Sit! Make yourselves comfortable!"

Kit looked around for a place to sit, but all the booths were taken. Possum Ansel immediately jumped from behind the counter and shooed the skinny pigeon from his booth.

"Hey, I was sitting there!" the pigeon objected.

"You've been there an hour and had one cheese ale and half a cracker!" the possum scolded him. "These folks are heroes, and they're hungry for real food!"

"Sorry, Ned," Uncle Rik apologized to the pigeon, even as he slid into the pigeon's seat.

"Sorry don't smooth my feathers," the pigeon grumbled and strutted out of the store in a huff. Kit felt bad about taking the bird's table from him.

"Don't worry about Blue Neck Ned," Uncle Rik told him. "He'll find some other place to perch. Always does."

"I'll get cooking on those casseroles," said Possum Ansel. "And you folks enjoy yourselves. Fresh acorn bread for the table?"

"Please," said Kit. He loved acorn bread when his mom made it, and he was happy to taste one small reminder of home.

"Otis, darling, bring these fellows some fresh acorn bread," Ansel called, and Otis lumbered back into the kitchen.

Once they were alone at the table, Uncle Rik leaned in close to Kit and Eeni. "I need to go talk to that badger for a minute," he whispered. "You two eat up. Enjoy yourselves, and I'll be back soon, okay?"

"Okay," said Kit, eagerly watching the kitchen door for the arrival of his snack and glad they might get some protection on their side. Strength ruled in Ankle Snap Alley, and Kit and Eeni had more brains to offer than brawn.

Uncle Rik scurried into the back room, leaving Eeni and Kit to themselves again.

"So . . . *that* was exciting," said Eeni.

"That was terrifying," said Kit.

"That's life here in Ankle Snap." Eeni shrugged. "It's a wild place. You walk out the door, and you never know what'll happen next."

"I don't know if I'll ever get used to it."

"An animal can get used to anything," Eeni told him.

"We're no house pets here. We adapt to the world; we don't expect the world to adapt to us."

"I never thought about it like that before," said Kit.

"See? Already thinking in new ways." Eeni smirked. "This here alley is an education and a half!"

"I guess . . . but, don't you go to school too?"

Eeni shrugged. "My school's the mud and mystery of life beneath the Slivered Sky."

"You mean, you don't go to, like, regular—?"

Eeni cut him off with a wave of her paw. "I don't want to talk about it," she said.

"Sorry." Kit blushed.

"Don't worry about it," Eeni told him. "By the way . . . I'm real sorry about your parents."

"Yeah." Kit wiped his eye with his paw. "Like you said . . . we adapt. It's what wild animals do."

Eeni nodded. "You're a quick learner, Kit."

"I sort of have to be now that I'm an orphan," he told her. "But I made my mother a promise, and if I can figure out what's so important about this clue, then I'll be able to—"

Just then, a loud clatter interrupted him, followed by crashing noise. He'd barely cocked his ears in the direction of the kitchen, when Uncle Rik came flying backward through the door and smashed into three heaping plates of piping-hot trash casserole. An instant later, Otis came flying through the door and smashed into the pastry case, crushing all the liver cakes and marrow cookies into crumbs.

The customers gasped and cried out. Possum Ansel froze in place once more. Uncle Rik groaned on the ground, and Otis stood up from the wrecked case and flexed his fists. He charged back into the kitchen.

Faster than a hummingbird's wink, the badger came flying back out of the kitchen again just as Uncle Rik stood up again, and the big fellow landed flat on top of the dazed raccoon, smashing them both back down into the ruined pastry case. This time badger and raccoon were knocked out cold.

And then Kit heard the tinkling of a tiny bell.

Ding-ding-ding.

His blood froze in his veins. A large orange cat slipped into the dining room and licked the baking sugar from his front paw.

Sixclaw.

The cat glanced around the room and grinned. "Business is closed for the night," the cat said. "Everyone out."

The customers popped to their paws, feet, and claws and bolted through the front door. The possum played possum still; the badger and Uncle Rik lay side by side on the ground, and the cat fixed his yellow gaze on Kit and Eeni.

"You, Kit, I'd kindly ask to stick around," the cat me-owed, although his meow was about as cute and cuddly as a sack of rusted razor blades.

"You . . . you . . . ," Kit stammered.

"Oh, Kit." The cat chuckled. "It's a pleasure to meet you again. Or, should I say, *eat* you again. This is a restaurant after all, and I'd love some Kit casserole."

Chapter Fourteen

THE PARISH SCRIBE

SIXCLAW smoothed his ears with his paw, flashing all six of his claws at the same time. Eeni glanced to the restaurant door, then back to the cat again, which seemed to amuse him.

"Try to run and I'll be burping up your bones before your paws hit the floor," he said.

Kit jumped from the booth and pulled the garbage-can-lid tabletop up with him, holding it like a shield. He put himself and his shield in front of Eeni without hesitation. "You leave her alone," he barked.

The cat burst into a fit of laughter. "He-he, ha-ha! What a sight! Honor among vermin!" The cat's laughter stopped as suddenly as it started. "Too bad it won't save you."

With one paw, Sixclaw grabbed a broken shard of the pastry case from the floor and tossed the glass at Kit's table-shield. Kit batted the projectile away, which left part of his right side exposed. The cat's other paw lashed out, swiping so fast Kit barely had time to leap backward to avoid being gutted on the spot. He tripped over Eeni, and they both tumbled to the floor on their backs, Kit still holding the shield over them.

Sixclaw's swipe left six red gashes across the light gray fur of Kit's belly, but before he even felt the sting of the wound, the cat pounced. He slammed his weight down onto the shield, pinning Kit beneath it. Eeni squirmed free to avoid being suffocated in his fur.

She saw a book of People's matches that Ansel used to burn the sugar on top of his sweet and savory sardine brûlée, and she dove for it.

Just before Eeni's paw gripped one of the wooden fire sticks, Sixclaw jabbed one claw clean through her tail, pinning her in place, while the rest of him still held Kit down.

"Ahh!" Eeni screamed. The matches were just out of reach.

"I think no fire for you, little rat," Sixclaw told her. "You Wild Ones are not supposed to have People's things, and I do hate the smell of singed fur." He dug his claw deeper into her tail, and she did her best not to scream again, still straining to reach the matches. With one flick of his tail, Sixclaw swished them away from her and turned his attention back to Kit. "I fear you are out of tricks, young one. And now it's time to die."

He opened his mouth, showing his fangs, just as sharp and deadly as his claws, but before he could bite down on Kit's neck, he was struck in the face with a shining brown acorn.

"What in the soggy sardine was that?" The cat turned, just in time to get another acorn in the eye, and then another right between the eyes. "Ow!" he yelled, and Kit used the distracted moment to heave up the shield and knock Sixclaw off him.

The cat released Eeni too, as he had to jump away from a sudden barrage of hard acorns aimed straight for his head at high velocity. "Ah! Stop it, you vermin," he shouted, seeking shelter behind the ruins of the counter he'd destroyed, and finding none, continued to leap this way and that, hit over and over again by an unceasing hail of nuts.

Kit saw the source of his salvation: six mice, their robes

bright white, manning tiny catapults made from mouse-traps, and behind them, in a straight line to the front door, six *more* mice, passing acorns in to the firing squad, so they would never run out of ammunition. Sixclaw was pressed against the back of the shop, cowering and covering his head with his forepaws.

One of the mice stepped forward and raised a tiny fist. The barrage of nuts ceased, and Sixclaw peered through his fingers at his assailant.

"I am Martyn of the Church Mice, Chief Scribe of this parish, and you, Sixclaw, are trespassing. Begone now or face our wrath!"

Kit recognized the mouse from the alley. This was the one who'd handed him the pamphlet.

Sixclaw lowered his paws to the ground so he stood again on all fours. "You and your kind've no right to this alley. It was loaned to you for seven hundred and seven seasons and those seven hundred and seven seasons are up."

"No," said the mouse. "We know there was another deal, between Azban, the First Raccoon, and Brutus, Duke of Dogs. Brutus made a bet and lost, and our mousecestors were the scribes who signed the deal upon the Bone of Contention. The deal gives the Wild Ones the right to this turf for all time."

"And if this Bone was real, you'd have showed it generations ago," scoffed the cat.

"The Bone is real," Martyn replied calmly. "And you are in no position to argue."

The cat's big yellow eyes stared at the mouse, his bell dinged, and he spat on the ground. "Choke on cheese, church mouse!"

Martyn lowered his fist, and another hail of nuts pelted Sixclaw.

"Ahh, enough, enough," the cat yelled. "Fine!"

Martyn raised his fist and the barrage stopped.

"Know this, vermin," the cat shouted so that even the cowering animals outside the shop could hear him. "Without that Bone, you've no proof you belong here. Any of you who are still in Ankle Snap Alley in two days' time will face the wrath of the Flealess. Not even your gang of Rascals will keep us from driving you out of this place forever."

"I have a counteroffer," said Martyn. "You tell the Flealess *they* are not welcome here in Ankle Snap Alley anymore. Not a cat, not a dog, not so much as a hamster. This is a place for the Wild Ones, and any house pet who dares disturb us again will be in violation of the ancient treaties and will face dire consequences."

"I eat mice like you for breakfast!" the cat hissed, but he turned to leave through the back door, the way he'd come. Just before exiting, he stopped. His tail swished against the ceiling, and he spoke over his shoulder. "There won't always be someone to save you, Kit. We'll meet again, and I promise, it will be painful."

"Go!" Martyn shouted.

The cat left the restaurant, meowing sweetly as he strolled away, his tiny bell tinkling.

The mouse turned to Kit. "You're bleeding."

"My uncle is hurt worse," said Kit. "I think the cat knocked him out. And Eeni's tail could use a bandage probably."

"My acolytes will tend to their wounds," Martyn said.

"Your what?" Kit had never heard that word before, and he feared Martyn would be another fast-talking alley creature.

"Ac-o-lytes," Martyn repeated slowly. "It means my followers. They are members of my faith, and you can trust them with your friends. Not only have they studied the healers' textbooks, they wrote them. We mice do all the writing here. But now you must come with me. We haven't much time to lose. If we do not find the Bone of Contention, all our arguments will be for naught. It is the only proof we have that our kind belongs here. Come along!"

"Our kind?" Kit wondered. "We're not the same kind, though. You're a mouse."

"We are all mice in the eyes of—" Martyn began to

recite. "Oh, never mind, what I mean is, we're all wild so we're all in this together against the Flealess. Now come on!" He grabbed Kit by the jacket and tried to tug him out of the bakery.

Kit just looked down at him, unmoving.

"Hey, mouse," Eeni interjected, even as she clutched her bleeding tail in her paw. "Wherever Kit goes, I go. We made a promise. Howl to snap."

"If you wish, young lady." Martyn let go of Kit's jacket and brushed himself off. "Perhaps it is for the best if we go together. We are going to see a friend of yours . . . well, one friend who is many friends."

Eeni seemed to understand what the mouse meant, though Kit didn't. She dropped her tail and her arms hung at her sides. "You mean . . . ?"

Martyn took a deep breath. "We have an appointment," he said.

"With who?" Kit wondered.

"With *whom*," corrected Eeni.

"With the Rat King," Martyn said.

"The Rat King doesn't make appointments." Eeni shook her head. "The Rat King hasn't had an appointment in hundreds of seasons. Everyone knows that."

"Three hundred and twenty-four seasons, to be precise," said Martyn. "Which is when my great-great-great-

great-great-great-great-great-grandmouse made this very appointment. So I think we should not keep him waiting any longer, don't you?"

"I guess not," said Kit. "But . . . uh, who is the Rat King?"

Chapter Fifteen

ONE-HUNDRED-HEADED CANNIBAL

THE Rat King was not exactly a king, and was not exactly a rat either.

The Rat King was, in fact, a hundred rats, whose tails were so tangled and whose fur was so thick and knotted that all one hundred rats had become impossibly stuck together. A hundred rats who moved as one body, spoke as one voice, but saw a hundred different ways.

The Rat King never ruled over the rats, nor ruled over

anything at all, actually. Nobody knew why it came to be known as the Rat King, but since as far back as anyone could remember and farther back than that still, there had been a Rat King in the city under the Slivered Skies.

The Rat King was born by accident countless seasons ago. Two rats fighting over a piece of rotten fruit found their tails hopelessly tangled. They kept fighting, but neither could win and neither could retreat. They would have fought each other to the death, if a third rat hadn't come along to break them up and gotten herself tangled too.

The fighting rats felt so bad they'd tangled an innocent peacekeeping rat into their fight that they vowed to cooperate together so that there would be enough food for all three of them. They grew to live in such harmony that other rats came along, wanting to join their tangle. The Rat King was seen as a peaceful, joyous, cooperative way of living, and rats from all over the city raced to escape the struggles of survival and tangled themselves in the Rat King.

To prevent all of ratkind from becoming a single mass of tangled rats, the Rat King agreed with itself to limit its number to one hundred rats at a time. When one rat got too old, a young rat took its place, bringing the energy and ideas of youth to the perspective of the Rat King. That way, many generations were a part of the Rat King at the same time, male and female, young and old.

"But what happens to the old rat?" Kit asked as they made their way beside Martyn to the end of the alley.

"It gets absorbed into the Rat King," said Martyn.

"Absorbed? How?"

"Can we not talk about this?" Eeni snapped. The whole topic seemed to make her very uncomfortable.

"It's best not to think too deeply about it," Martyn agreed.

"You mean . . . the old rat gets . . . eaten? By the other rats?" Kit stopped where he stood.

Martyn nodded. "In a sense, it gets eaten by itself."

"Gross!" Kit cried out. "So we're going to see a giant, hundred-headed cannibal rat?"

"Perspective is not easy to get nor easy to keep," Martyn explained. "It often comes at a terrible price. The Rat King knows more and sees more and remembers more than any other creature under the moon, but for this knowledge, it has spent countless seasons devouring itself."

"That's mad!" Kit couldn't believe it.

"Yes, some believe the Rat King has gone mad," Martyn agreed. "But in times of madness, it is the wisdom of madness we seek."

"You know about this Rat King?" Kit asked Eeni.

Eeni kicked at the dirt with her back paw, then studied the wound in her tail. "Yeah," she said without looking up at him. "I know about it. All rats do. It's . . . our culture."

"Oh," said Kit, feeling guilty for calling her culture gross.

Eeni shrugged. "Just because I'm a rat doesn't mean I like everything rats do. You like everything raccoons do?"

"I didn't know raccoons did anything not to like until I met the Blacktail brothers," Kit said.

"Well, don't be so quick to count another fella's fleas," Eeni said. "It's a big world, and every creature's got his own."

"You are a young philosopher!" Martyn clapped his paws. "I am amazed you do not attend Saint Rizzo's Academy for Gifted Rodents.

"I did school once," Eeni said. "It wasn't for me."

"So you quit Saint Rizzo's?" The mouse seemed dismayed.

"What's it to ya, church mouse?" Eeni crossed her arms. "School quit me. They didn't much want a rat with a bad attitude and a talent for thieving. Now can we get going or what? We don't have a lot of time to find this Bone, do we?"

"Yes, yes, of course," Martyn grumbled, gathering his robes about himself and scurrying on, clearly flustered by the young rat's bad attitude. Kit didn't know much about life in the city, but from what he'd seen, he was pretty sure mice and rats didn't get along.

As they made their way toward the large Dumpster at the end of the alley, where the Scavengers' Market bustled, creatures popped their heads from their homes and shops to gawk at Kit, Eeni, and Martyn. Whispers passed from mole to squirrel to ferret to hedgehog. Young chipmunks pointed and hid their faces in their mothers' fur, while a group of teenaged news finches perched in the bush by the entrance to the market, chirping out the evening's stories.

"Ansel's Trashed by Carnivorous Kitty!" one finch cried.

"Church Mice Squeak and Cat Goes Shriek!" another shouted.

"Flealess Give Two Nights Until Eviction! Time to Start Packing?" chirped a third.

"Extra! Extra! Who's the Raccoon the Cat Was After? Who's the Cause of All the Trouble? Finch's Nightly News Has the Scoop!" cried out a fourth.

"Hey, pal!" the first finch yelled down to Kit. He wore his hat cocked low on his head, so he could only see with one eye. It gave him a cool, insouciant look. Kit wished he had that kind of confidence. "How's about an interview? The folks are dying to know about you. You really think you can find the Bone of Contention?"

"I, uh, don't know . . . ," Kit said, nervously adjusting his own hat.

"Extra! Extra!" the finches shouted together. "Young Raccoon Denies All Knowledge! What's He Hiding? Hear All About It!"

"But I didn't deny anything," Kit objected. "I don't *know* anything."

"Ignore them," Eeni said. "They're no better than Mrs. Costlecrunk and her brood. The finches just charge for their gossip and call it news. You'll do well not to listen to a word they say."

"Okay," Kit said, walking on.

Together, they passed by the bustling Scavengers' Market, where stray dogs eyed them suspiciously.

"Don't stare at them," Eeni warned. "They're with the Rabid Rascals, just like Basil and the Blacktail brothers. And they all know by now what you did to those three hoodlums."

"What *I* did?" Kit couldn't believe his ears. "They cheated me and tried to feed me to a snake!"

Eeni nodded. "And you stopped them. Nobody stands up to the Rabid Rascals like that. You'll have to watch your back."

"Cats after me and news birds after me and now a pack of gangsters after me too?" Kit whined. "I've only been here one night!"

"At least you're having an adventure," Eeni said. "You can't say life here's boring, can you?"

Kit did not find Eeni's perspective very comforting.

"Anyway," said Eeni, "I think a group of gangsters is called a trouble. A trouble of gangsters."

"Not a pack?" Kit wondered.

"A pack's just for dogs," she said.

"How do you know all this?" Kit asked her.

"I guess school wasn't totally useless."

Martyn tapped her on the shoulder and pointed to a hole in the fence that cut off Ankle Snap Alley from one of the People's streets. "This way!"

"The Rat King doesn't live here in the alley?" Kit asked.

"The city beneath the Slivered Sky is much larger than one alley, young Kit," the mouse explained. "And the Rat King has lived in every corner of it."

Chapter Sixteen

GIVE A HOOT

BEYOND the edge of the alley, Kit and Eeni had to scurry across the big pavement river following Martyn, whose white robes glowed as he passed through the pools of electric light. They scampered along the edge of a square brick building where the People worked all day, past giant metal doors, and beneath a big brown truck.

The mouse stopped at the edge of a rotted pier that jutted out over black water. Kit was shocked to smell the sea salt air. He hadn't known they were so close to an ocean. The pier was cut off from the concrete by a razor-wire fence, but there was a burrow hole dug under it, big enough for a dozen mice or one young raccoon to squeeze through. Martyn gestured for Kit to climb under first, but just as he touched his snout to the ground, an owl hooted from above.

"Whooo goes below?" the owl demanded. Kit looked up and saw a big brown owl perched atop the fence. Its mighty talons wrapped around the razor wire as if it were the harmless branch of a tree. Like Eeni had said, Wild Ones adapt. The owl wore a crisp black suit and blinked his wide yellow eyes behind dark glasses. "Whooo are yooou?"

Eeni froze in place. It was a well-known fact that rats did not like owls on account of owls having rats for dinner on a regular basis.

"Uh . . . uh . . . ," Eeni stammered.

She glanced around. Martyn the mouse had vanished. Brave as they might appear, mice were also terrified of owls. They usually ended up as breakfast.

Kit, however, was far too big for an owl to eat for any meal, and besides, he knew owls from back home, so he stood up on his hind feet, pressed the tips of his front paws together in greeting, and turned the question right back on the bird who was asking it. "Who are *you*?"

The owl swiveled his head to peer down at Kit. He blinked once.

"I am the bouncer, you impudent masked scoundrel!"

the owl cried out. Kit noticed that the owl used the word *impudent* when he could have just said *rude*. Owls back under the Big Sky were like that too . . . always using big words when little ones would've done just fine. As if being impossible to understand made them wise. Real wisdom, Kit's father always told him, didn't need to hide behind big words.

Kit figured owls in the city under the Slivered Sky were the same as owls out in the trees of the Big Sky. If you made them feel smart, they'd let you do anything.

"I didn't mean to be rude, sir," Kit replied. "And I don't understand them big words you use. I never meant to be *in pudding . . .*"

"'Impudent,'" the owl corrected him, just as Kit knew he would. "'In pudding'? Ha! Unlikely."

"Yes, sir, *impudent*, I meant to say." Kit looked down at his feet. "Could you forgive a poor raccoon for not knowing such smart words? I never had much schooling, sir."

"Sir, indeed!" The owl puffed out his chest.

"I apologize for troubling you," Kit said. "You must have more important things to do than talk to a young raccoon and his friend."

The owl swiveled his head around in a circle. "I do indeed! My college of owls is waiting for me to start our card game."

"Well, we don't mean to keep your college waiting," Kit said. "You see, we have an appointment to see the Rat King."

The owl hooted in surprise. "An appointment? Ha! An owl has stood sentry for the Rat King since this whole area was nothing but stone and beach, and in that time, there has not been one appointment!"

"If you'll just check, sir . . . ," Kit suggested.

The owl blinked in annoyance, but one of his talons reached into the pocket of his suit jacket and produced a small scroll, which he proceeded to unfurl, letting it sail all the way to the ground. Kit noticed that the giant sheet of paper was completely blank, but for one line at the top. "And your name is?"

"Kit, sir. I believe a mouse made the appointment some time ago . . ."

The owl's eyes moved painfully slowly across the single line at the top of the scroll.

"Very well, *Kit*," the owl finally said. "A raccoon *does* have an appointment, although whether or not that raccoon is you is hard to say."

"It's me," said Kit.

"It's *I*," corrected the owl. "You are the subject of the sentence, therefore you should use the subject pronoun *I* rather than the object pronoun *me*."

"Yep," said Kit. "If you say so. It's I."

"I do say so." The owl nodded, and Kit smiled. The owl had just agreed that Kit was the raccoon on the list.

"So?" asked Kit. "Since we agree I'm the raccoon on your list, can I go in now, please?"

"Well . . ." The owl scratched his head with one talon, puzzled about how exactly he'd just agreed or what exactly he had agreed to. "You are perhaps a hundred seasons late, Kit."

"Sorry, sir," Kit apologized. "I couldn't help it. I wasn't born a hundred seasons ago."

"Excuses," the owl grumbled, as he began rolling up his scroll. "But you two may enter. And bring your mouse friend. He thinks I don't see him, but I certainly do."

Martyn slowly revealed himself from beneath a pile of bricks, looking bashful. He'd found a crumb from a Person's lunch and was quietly munching on it.

Kit's stomach grumbled to remind him how hungry he still was.

The owl, keen of hearing as well as sight, smirked and called out to Kit as he turned away. "You know, those friends of yours would make a fine snack for a growing lad like you. A lot of vitamins in a rodent."

Eeni squeaked, and Kit gasped.

Where he was from, it was not polite to suggest eating one's friends, and he assumed the same was true in the city. Beneath all their big words, owls were just big rude birds, and he was glad to put this one behind him, although he did understand that if the Rat King wanted to keep away trespassers, an owl at the gate was certainly an effective way to do it.

Kit let Eeni and Martyn go under the fence ahead of him, both of them shuddering beneath the owl's cold yellow stare.

They scurried beside the pier and reached a crumbling wall with faded writing in the People's language along the side of it. There were broken windows high in the brick at one end. The other end had collapsed and lay open to the sea, where all kinds of driftwood and flotsam had washed up into it.

"We're here," Martyn announced.

"What is this place?" Kit asked.

"The People called it a public pool," Martyn explained. "In the warm season, they would come here in special clothing and swim in a false lake they built inside, just beside the real ocean."

"They built a false lake, right beside the ocean?" Kit couldn't imagine why People would do such a thing, when they could swim in the ocean whenever they wanted. But perhaps, when you've covered the world in cities of glass and concrete so tall that only slivers of sky can be seen from the ground, you forget about oceans.

"They abandoned this long ago," Martyn said. "It has been the home of the Rat King for quite some time."

"So . . . uh . . . do we just go in?" Kit asked.

"No one goes in without an appointment," Martyn said. "Many a creature has tried, and none has ever come out again."

"But"—Kit gulped—"we have an appointment. The owl said so."

"No," Martyn corrected him. "The owl said you have an appointment, and you alone. We will wait outside until you return."

"But I don't even know why I'm going to see him."

"The Rat King isn't a *him*," Eeni declared. "The Rat King is made up of boys *and* girls."

"But it isn't called the Rat *Queen*," Kit said.

"Well, maybe it should be—" Eeni answered him.

"Please, children," Martyn interrupted. "We have no time to debate this. Kit, you must go. The Rat King will know about this footprint you carry. It is our only hope to find the Bone of Contention before the Flealess evict us from Ankle Snap. It is the only way we will avoid terrible bloodshed. Please, go in." Martyn gestured to the rusted fence and Kit took a hesitant step forward.

Eeni moved to follow him again, but Martyn blocked her path.

"He must go alone," Martyn said. "No exceptions."

"But I made a promise," Eeni said.

The mouse didn't move. Kit looked back at Eeni, worry bristling from every whisker on his face.

"I'll be right here when you get back," she promised him. "I still need to school you on so much. I promise. Howl to snap." She held up her little paws in an A.

Kit held up his own paws in return. "Howl to snap," he repeated, then scuttled into the dark of the abandoned building.

"Oh, Kit," Eeni called, "tell the Rat King something for me."

"What's that?" Kit waited.

Eeni chewed her lip, thought a moment, and then said, "Tell the Rat King that Eeni, from the Nest at Broke Track Junction, says she's sorry."

Kit scrunched his eyebrows, puzzled by the message, but the expression of worry and embarrassment on Eeni's face made him decide not to ask what she meant. She knew, and that was enough. Friends, he decided, let each other keep the secrets they need to keep. It'd be up to Eeni if she wanted to tell Kit what she meant.

So he just responded, "I'll tell the Rat King—I'll tell *her*."

Eeni smiled and Kit crept away into the dark.

Chapter Seventeen

THE RATS
REMEMBER

THE air smelled of wet fur and of salt water, sewage, and rotting fruit. Beneath it, a hint of old chemicals. The People were obsessed with cleaning things, dousing their spaces in soaps and perfumes until nothing could live, but of course, the moment the People abandoned their places, life came roaring back. Vines grew on the walls, flowers burst from the broken floor tiles, and succulent insects skittered in the cracks. This dark building was teeming with life, and

Kit's stomach grumbled again. He wondered if he had time to stop and eat a grub or two.

Martyn's words echoed in Kit's mind. *No one goes in without an appointment. Many a creature has tried, and none has ever come out again.*

He decided it was best not to keep the Rat King waiting any longer.

He made his way along the wall in the dark, his claws scraping against the tile. Every step he took made a loud *click, click, click.*

He passed a row of rusted metal cubbies, some with doors half off their hinges, some shut and barred with metal locks. He was tempted to stop and pick open a lock, see what goodies he could find, but there were signs posted along the walls and on the doors of the cubbies. He couldn't read the words, but one had a picture of a rat stenciled on it, and below, a word of the People's language that all the wild creatures learned to recognize when they were young: POISON.

This was a place of danger, for People and animals alike.

Kit took a gentle step on a pile of dried leaves and heard a snap. His paw rested on something metal, not tile, and he had a split second to dive out of the way as a cage snapped up from the floor around him. He rolled just in time and the trap caught only air.

He looked at the metal grate of the cage, rusted but

thick, and the hinges, still strong. He'd have to be more careful where he placed his paws. Where there was one trap, there were always more to follow.

Kit entered a giant room. The roof had collapsed so the stars above were visible. One streak of moonlight cut the space and drew a circle on the bottom of the large pit that filled most of the floor. This was the lake the People had built inside, but it was dry now, and at its deepest end, in the shadow outside the moonlight, something stirred.

"Come, come, young one, we've waited and waited and waited for you," a voice—or rather, a hundred voices all together in a rat chorus—said. Kit could only see the shape, a writhing shadow of fur and tail, with two hundred red eyes. "Step where we can see you. Hurry now, son of Azban."

The voices were young and old, male and female, rough and smooth. Blended together, they sounded older than moonlight.

Kit hesitated, but figured the only rat he'd met so far had been good to him, so maybe he could trust this one too. He climbed down the steps at the opposite end and crawled warily deeper. As he moved, he heard a loud chewing noise. The deeper he got, the louder the chewing sounded. He noticed the bones of small animals littering the floor. All along the high walls of the dry concrete lake were the skeletons of rats. Kit bit his tongue to keep from screaming.

When he reached the pool of moonlight, the Rat King called for him to stop and the chewing sounds ceased. "Stay there, young Kit. Let's look at you."

Kit stopped and the hair on his back prickled. It was a strange feeling to know that a hundred pairs of eyes were studying him. The sound of gnawing, chewing, and crunching returned, broken by distinct voices.

"*He looks frightened,*" whispered one small rat voice from the mass of rats.

"*Of course he's frightened,*" added another. "*He should be frightened.*"

"*But he's come nonetheless. His fear does not control him.*"

"*Rather brave, that is.*"

"*I want popcorn.*"

The Rat King was talking to itself. It was like listening to someone's thoughts, if all their thoughts had to be spoken out loud.

"*Me too! I'm hungry!*" one more added.

"*Focus! Is this one brave enough to find the Bone?*"

"*His parents were brave.*"

"*Brave is not a who. Brave is a what.*"

"*What you do, not who you are.*"

"*What did his parents do?*"

"*His parents got killed.*"

"*The Flealess kill the brave and cowardly alike.*"

"But will they kill Kit?"

"I want popcorn!"

"Excuse me." Kit interrupted the Rat King's discussion with itself. "I can hear you, you know. I'm, like, right here."

"Yes, you are," the Rat King spoke again in one voice. "And we do not know what to make of you, Kit. We knew one day you would come, but we did not know who you would be when you arrived."

"Can you see the future?" Kit tried to peer into the dark at the mystical Rat King. If there was a creature in the world that saw the future and chose not to warn folks like Kit when tragedy was coming, that creature had a lot to answer for. To see disaster coming for others and do nothing to stop it struck Kit as just plain mean.

"We cannot see the future," the Rat King replied. "We can simply see more than most and remember most of all. We hold the memories of generations in our mind, and so we knew that one of your kind would come to us one day, as one always comes. History turns and turns, but the future changes very little from the past until someone brave comes along to change it. We wonder if you are that someone."

"I'd rather change the past than the future," said Kit. "I want my parents back."

The Rat King sighed a hundred putrid sighs.

"Touching," said one rat.

"*Beautiful,*" said another.

"But impossible," said all the voices together. "Your past is as attached to you as your tail. It follows you and keeps you balanced, but it cannot lead you forward. Yet there are other creatures with other parents who will die if a war comes to Ankle Snap Alley. You can prevent their pasts from bearing the same scars as yours. Do you want to help these others?"

"Of course," said Kit, without hesitation.

"*He is kind,*" said one rat voice.

"*He is* brave *and kind,*" said another.

"*Popcorn,*" said a third.

"*We'll eat later!*" shouted one more. "*Time is running out!*"

"Time for what?" Kit asked.

"Don't interrupt us while we're thinking!" the Rat King yelled.

"Sorry," said Kit. "But you really need to stop speaking in riddles." He pulled the stone from his pouch and held it up toward the shadow. "Would you please just explain this to me so I can do what I promised my mother I would do?"

The massive shape of the Rat King shifted. It swung wide around the edge of the moonlight and shoved its hundred faces into the glow, towering high over Kit. Two hundred red rat eyes blazed at him, and two hundred rat-sharp front teeth shined from one hundred bristling brown and black and white and gray faces, and every face looked wild with madness.

"The Footprint of Azban!" the Rat King hissed.

"Uh, yeah," said Kit, whose patience for the Rat King had worn as thin as pig's hair. "Can you tell me something I don't already know about?"

"This footprint was left by Azban to mark the place where the Bone of Contention was hidden for future generations." The Rat King paused dramatically, but Kit simply waited. He tapped his foot.

"He didn't oooh," said one rat.

"He didn't ahhh," said another.

"No sense of drama," said a third. *"Just tell him the rest."*

"Long ago, when the First People left and the New People built their city, they brought with them their pets," the Rat King went on. "Dogs and cats and birds more comfortable with the People's ways than with the animals they once were. The New People had long ago forgotten our languages and ignored our societies, but their pets remembered. And the pets feared that the Wild Ones, who lived off the human scraps and scroungings, would ruin their comfy lives by turning the People against all the animals. So they tried to rid the city of our kind, killing rats and mice, raccoon and rabbit, deer and bear and boar and hawk and dove and all else they could find. The cats soon joined them, and we were nearly driven to extinction.

"But the wild creatures joined together, fought back, and a great battle raged for years, with many dead on all sides. The Wild Ones feared that all was lost, and so they signed a truce. They could live in the narrow places of the People's towns, the hidden edges and dark corners, places like Ankle Snap Alley, for seven hundred and seven seasons. When the seven hundred and seven were over, they were to go into exile and give the pets all the land that lay beside the People. The deal was struck, and the Wild Ones and Flealess lived in temporary peace."

"Until the truce ran out," said Kit.

"Yes, this very season," said the Rat King. "But there are rumors of a secret deal, made long ago by Azban and Brutus, the Duke of Dogs, who was the pride of the People's mayor. The raccoon and the dog played a game of cards one night that lasted into the next day and the night after and on after that some more. For two suns and three moons they played, Azban betting away everything the Wild Ones had, until he proposed a final bet, the right to Ankle Snap Alley for all time, for all the Wild Ones to live in freedom from the Flealess forever.

"Of course, Brutus, who had been winning the whole time, agreed, and Azban called the mice to draw up the deal. They inscribed it onto the shinbone of a mighty elk, and Azban, who'd planned the whole thing from the beginning, won the final bet. Brutus flew into a rage, accused Azban of cheating. The big dog tore the room apart and nearly killed everyone present, except the brave raccoon fled with Brutus on his trail and hid the Bone where Brutus couldn't get it, too low to dig and too high to reach, caged with iron light and locked in threes."

"'Caged with iron light'? What does *that* mean?" Kit asked, but the Rat King ignored him, caught up in the momentum of the story.

"Azban swore to the dog that before the seven hundred seven seasons were done, one of his kind would return and show everyone what had been won, that all animals would live side by side in peace.

"And that is why raccoons in the city have always searched and scrounged, looking for the Bone inscribed by their ancestor. That is why your parents gave their lives to find it, and that is why you must follow this footprint where it leads, to find the Bone before the final season has ended."

Silence fell again, and Kit thought long and hard about his ancestor and his parents and the task now before him. Finally, he asked the question he should've asked from the start: "So where's the footprint lead? What's too low to dig and too high to reach, caged with iron light and locked in threes?"

"No patience, this one," said one rat.

"No respect for gravitas!" said another.

"Sooner he's gone, the sooner we eat," said a third.

"We don't know what those words mean," said the Rat King. "Azban did love tricks. But the painting on this stone beside the footprint is a People's mark, painted by a juvenile in more recent times than Azban walked. The People's young sometimes mark their territory with paint the way a wolf marks with his spray. They call it 'graffiti.' This mark we have seen before in our travels. It is from a dark and dangerous place, below the city."

"Below?" Kit gulped.

"The sewers," said the Rat King. "A more dangerous place there could not be. A hungry beast lurks below, devouring the flesh of all who set claw on her turf . . . but that is where this footprint leads, brave Kit, and that is where you'll have to go." The Rat King tilted perilously high over Kit's head. "Be brave and change the future," all its voices declared. "Or be fearful and repeat the past. Only you can decide."

The Rat King pulled away quickly toward a hole on the far wall of the pool and vanished as suddenly as it had appeared. Kit stood alone in the circle of moonlight, surrounded by the skeletons of generations of royal rats. It was amazing how all those rats remembered so much, amazing how memory really was like magic, able to bring the distant past to life and illuminate a path to the future. He wished his memory were that good. He found he could barely remember what his own mother looked like.

He'd forgotten something else too, he realized.

"Oh no! Your . . . uh . . . Highness? I forgot to tell you something," he called out into the darkness. "Eeni, from the Nest at Broke Track Junction, says she's sorry." His voice echoed. He didn't know if the Rat King could hear him or if it was even listening anymore.

But through the long silence, one rat voice whispered back: *"Tell her, her mother forgives her."*

"'Her mother'?" Kit said.

His jaw dropped.

Of course.

No wonder Eeni was so upset about the Rat King. Eeni's mother had joined the Rat King. That's why Eeni didn't seem to have a family. That's why Eeni lived on the mean streets of Ankle Snap Alley.

He wanted to ask the lone voice more, but another rat cut her off.

"I want popcorn," it said, and the whole creature scurried deep into the crumbling walls, where Kit didn't dare to follow.

Chapter Eighteen

A RAT OF ACTION

KIT had so many thoughts burning in his brain, he worried he'd singe his fur. How was he supposed to go into the sewers if there was a dangerous beast living down there? How was he supposed to find the one spot this footprint came from once he was down there? And, most perplexing, what was he going to say to Eeni when he saw her again?

In a way, she was an orphan just like him, but in the weirdest way possible. Her mother was alive but had chosen not to be her mother anymore. How does any creature keep going after something like that? Kit was in awe of

Eeni. She might be small, but she sure was strong in ways Kit couldn't begin to fathom.

As he thought about her, he heard the sudden and un-mistakable sound of a trap snapping shut.

"Gah! Of all the—!" Eeni shouted.

Kit poked his head around the corner and saw the white rat sniffing at the wire mesh of a cage that had closed around her. Her little pink paws shook the door, annoyed more than frightened.

"You need some help?" Kit offered as gently as he could.

"No, I love being stuck in a stupid trap for the second time tonight," she grumbled.

Kit felt around for the release lever. This kind of trap had a release for the People to open it and reset it after it'd been used. It was pretty easy from the outside. If only *this* had been the kind of trap that had snared his mother.

But the Rat King was right. The past was past and couldn't be undone.

He pulled the lever back with both his paws, and the door to the trap fell open. Eeni stepped out.

"Thanks, Kit." Eeni squeezed his paw.

"So, I told the Rat King what you asked me to," he said.

"I know," Eeni replied. "I was listening."

"A pickpocket and an eavesdropper?" Kit laughed. "You're a shady character, Eeni."

She smiled. "Terribly disreputable."

"So . . . your . . . mother?"

"Yeah." Eeni sniffled. "She joined the Rat King when I was little. It's a family tradition. Her mother joined, and her mother's mother joined. I was studying to join too, but . . . I don't know. I was only doing it to see my mother again. But I'm different from her. I didn't want to be a part of the Rat King. I'm my own rat, you know? I don't want to be just one of a hundred pairs of eyes, one thought in a hundred thoughts. I want my voice to be my own."

"It seems like it'd be cool to be a part of something so ancient and wise," said Kit.

"Wise?" Eeni grunted. "The Rat King isn't wise. You ever know a crowd to be wise?"

"But it knew all about the Bone of Contention—"

"If it was really wise, it'd know what to do about it," said Eeni. "Knowing something and doing something are totally different things. Me? I'm a doer." She looked Kit up and down. "And I think you are too."

Kit nodded. "If finding this Bone can keep anyone else from losing their family, then that's what I want to do," Kit said.

"Howl to snap," said Eeni.

Kit looked at the trap gaping open in front of them. "Well, you've got the snap part down . . . now let's go make those house pets howl."

Eeni followed Kit back through the building, her white fur silhouetted against Kit's gray, careful to follow in his footsteps exactly.

Just before they stepped back outside into the moonlight, she let Kit go ahead alone. She turned back toward the home of the Rat King and spoke into the dark, hoping that of the hundred pairs of ears listening, one of them would hear her loud and clear. "Bye, Mom," she said. "I love you."

Then she scurried outside and ran straight into the coils of a very angry python, who was very eager for revenge.

Chapter Nineteen

THE BOSS'S BET

SSSSO nicccce to ssssee you again," Basil hissed at her.

The Blacktail brothers had Kit pressed up against the wall at the point of a fork, and two more Rabid Rascals, strays from the Scavengers' Market, held Martyn at bay with teeth bared.

"You shouldn't have welshed on our bet," Shane Blacktail told Kit. "And you shouldn't have tricked us into that tire."

"It was a terrible way to treat your cousins," Flynn added. "And an even worse way to treat the Rascals. We have a reputation to uphold."

"A reputation as cheats and thieves and bullies," Martyn scolded. "You should all be ashamed, robbing from your own kind when the Flealess threaten us all!"

"Yeah, yeah, yeah," Shane grunted. "We've heard your moralizing before, mouse. Keep your mouse trap shut or we'll smash it in a mousetrap!"

"Good one!" Flynn gave his brother a high five. "Now, we're taking you to the boss, and we'll see if we can't make an example of you, your friend, and your lousy, no-good liar of an uncle."

"An example?" Kit gulped.

"Oh yessss," said Basil. "Ankle Ssssnap Alley cannot think the Rabid Rasssscalssss are weak enough to be fooled by a child. You cannot wrong ussss without ssssuffering conssssequenccccessss."

"And your consequences will be very, very painful," said Shane.

"Of course they will," said Kit, who was getting pretty used to being threatened by now.

The boss of the Rabid Rascals lived at the end of Ankle Snap Alley in an abandoned van the People had long ago mounted on cinder blocks and forgotten. From the outside, it looked like a rusted heap with wooden boards for windows and vines covering the roof.

On the inside, however, it was a mansion for vermin.

The walls were draped with quilts of scrounged fabric; there were upholstered burrows for sleeping, decorated with ribbons and coins and all kinds of stolen bits and baubles.

The boss lived in the way back, behind a beaded curtain where a plastic pool had been filled with cool, clean water pilfered from the People's homes. He lounged in the water or on the sand scattered around the pool, which had also been hauled from some distant beach by his loyal minions.

No one knew how old the boss was or how long he had been the boss at all. In fact, no one knew much about him except that he was a turtle and that he'd made his first fortune fixing bird fights and rigging the bets. Some said he had escaped from a pet store as a baby, others said he'd been born in the sewers, and a few said he'd come from the sunny country down south and arrived in the city before the People's buildings had cut the sky to slivers.

On a few things all the stories about the boss agreed: He was old, he was tough as his shell, and he was ruthless. He had enemies, but he never had them for long.

"So don't bother begging for mercy," Shane told Kit, shoving him toward the curtain. "You won't get any."

Two bright green parakeets fluttered their wings and drew the curtain apart so Kit could pass through. He stood in the soft sand outside the pink plastic pool and saw Uncle Rik in a metal birdcage.

"Don't hurt the boy!" his uncle cried out when he saw Kit. "He's innocent in all this!"

"Innocent?" Flynn Blacktail cried. "He lost a bet, and instead of paying up, he tossed us on the train tracks!"

"You cheated him, so he cheated you," Uncle Rik replied. "It's the way of the wild."

"Not . . . our . . . way," a creaky old voice spoke slowly from the water. The wrinkled head of a turtle popped above the edge of the pool and peered at Kit. Its pale green face sagged, and its eyes were hooded with heavy lids. The turtle looked sleepy and not particularly menacing.

"That's right," said Shane. "*We* cheat."

And Flynn added, "We don't *get* cheated."

"The boy hassss to learn," Basil said.

"Yes . . . ," the turtle agreed. "He will learn . . . a . . . lesson."

"No," said Uncle Rik. "Not a lesson."

"Yes." The turtle nodded. "Time to call . . . the teacher."

Eeni gasped. "You can't. That's not—"

Basil squeezed her tighter, so no sound came out even as her mouth formed a scream.

"Wait? What?" Kit looked up at the turtle. "Who's the teacher?"

"Why, my boy, I am the teacher," a little porcupine in a bow tie announced as he came rolling out of the glove compartment. He carried a small satchel on his back, which he carefully removed and set on the ground before him. "Delighted to meet you, Kit."

The porcupine stuck out his paw for a shake, and Flynn jabbed Kit in the back with the fork to prod him forward. Kit shook hands with the porcupine.

"You're a teacher?" Kit wondered, looking back at Eeni squirming helplessly in the snake's grip. His uncle had crumpled into a ball in the cage, sobbing quietly. Martyn stood defiantly with his paws folded across his chest, but the little mouse's eyes darted nervously. Why was everyone so afraid of a teacher?

"I am not *a* teacher," the porcupine corrected Kit. "I am *the* teacher. You see, when someone needs to learn a lesson, I teach it to them." He smiled politely, then puffed up so his sharp quills flared out around him. "I fear it will be a long lesson for you, Kit, and you will not enjoy it. Shall we begin?"

Shane grabbed Kit from behind and held his arms tightly behind his back. The porcupine pulled one of his own quills from his side and tested its sharpness, then stepped up to Kit, tapping his snout with the glistening point of the quill. "Shall I pierce his ears or his nose first?"

"I would never . . . tell you how . . . to do . . . your work," the turtle said. "I ask only . . . that his screams . . .

echo. The lesson is for all . . . of Ankle Snap Alley . . . to hear and . . . to fear."

Kit looked around for help, but saw only the merciless stares of the Rabid Rascals gang. There were cruel Basil and the angry Blacktail brothers. The creepy frog who'd tried to sell Kit weapons was there, and so was the stoat who'd urged him to place his unfortunate bet on the shell-and-nut game. There was the skinny pigeon from Ansel's bakery, Blue Neck Ned, pecking at a plate of grubs. While he ate, he watched Kit with his side eye. The turtle climbed lazily from his pool, to stretch out on the sand while Kit got tortured. Kit's uncle was in a cage; Martyn was on the wrong side of two dogs' snarling snouts, and Eeni couldn't move in the merciless hug of the python.

No one but Kit could save Kit.

He felt the sharp point of the porcupine quill rise against his snout. "We'll start with the nose," said the teacher.

"Wait," Kit cried. "I know the Flealess are coming to kick you all out of the alley, but I can stop them. I can find the Bone of Contention."

The animals fell silent. The boss cocked his head, and then burst out laughing. The other Rabid Rascals laughed with him.

"It's true!" Kit shouted over the laughter. "I saw the Rat King."

"The Rat King . . . is a lunatic," the boss said.

"That Rat King has . . . uh . . ." Kit searched for the word. "Perspective. The Rat King sees more and remembers more than anyone could!"

"You want some free advice, lad?" the turtle asked him, but gave the advice without waiting for Kit's answer. "Never trust a nest of rats. If a hundred rats agree on something, you can be sure they've lost their minds. Ain't nothing in this wide world true for the same hundred. We're meant to be individuals, Kit, who do what we want and think what we want and get what we can get before some other guy gets it from us."

"But if you don't let me find the Bone of Contention, all the wild animals who live here will suffer."

The turtle stretched his long turtle neck from his shell. "Well, it looks like you'll be the first then." He nodded toward the porcupine to begin Kit's torture.

"So you're a leash lover?" Kit yelled out.

This time, the crowd of animals didn't laugh. The room fell so quiet you could have heard a mole cough on the other side of the world.

"Did you call me a leash lover?" the turtle snapped.

"Oh, you've done it now, lad," the teacher muttered and straightened his bow tie.

"You *are* a leash lover," Kit yelled again. "I could help you prove that this land belongs to the Wild Ones, but instead of listening, you do the Flealess's dirty work? You're worse than a house pet. You're a dumb old sewer-stinking leash lover!"

All eyes shifted from Kit to the turtle, whose pale green face looked paler and greener than ever. After a pause that felt as long as winter and twice as cold, the turtle spoke.

"Brave words for such a young lad," he said, suddenly speaking as fast as anyone. His whole slow-talking thing was just an act that fell away when he got mad. "I'll need some proof you can do what you say."

"I told you what the Rat King said," Kit explained.

"Words ain't much good as proof," said the turtle. "Words are cheap as dirt and twice as useless. Anyone can use words to say anything they want. But deeds, Kit. Deeds are a rare thing. A deed doesn't lie. A deed, when done, stands against a lie. Let the mice have words. It was deeds that made the world." The boss cleared his throat. "I propose another bet. If you win, you can go free with your friends. If you lose, I kill you all."

"But we can kill 'em all anyway, Boss," Shane objected. "We don't need no bet!"

"Shut your snout," the turtle snapped at him. "I'm talking to the young fella here. What do you say, Kit?"

"What's the bet? I can't agree before I know what it is."

"Simple," the turtle told him. "You go into the sewers and bring me back the Bone of Contention before sunup.

If you succeed, I'll let your friends go free. If you lose, well . . . school's in session."

The porcupine tapped his quill on Kit's snout and smirked.

The turtle waited for Kit's answer. Everyone waited.

"Is there really a beast down there?" Kit wondered.

"Of course not." The turtle laughed. "It's just Gayle." Kit exhaled with relief. "Although Gayle *is* an alligator," he added. "The biggest alligator ever to live in the sewers beneath the Slivered Sky."

"An alligator?" Kit gulped.

"And she's a mean one," the turtle said. "Best get going, Kit . . . The rooster will be crowing bedtime before you know it."

Chapter Twenty

TOOTHSOME

THE Blacktail brothers walked Kit to the sewer entrance by the train tracks, taunting him all the while.

"You ever seen an alligator, young pal of my paw?" asked Shane.

"Teeth sharper than sunlight," said Flynn. "And a bite so fast it'll snap your head off while your paws keep walking."

"Don't scare the lad, my brother," Shane replied with a sarcastic smile. "Alligators can smell fear. You aren't afraid of giant teeth that lurk below the sewer filth, are you, Kit? You aren't afraid of massive jaws and terrible fangs, are you, you mole-faced tick-for-brains?"

Shane and his brother laughed and laughed.

"Will you two be quiet?" Kit grumbled as he walked. The purple night was already starting to swell with red, and Kit knew that morning would be along soon. He wasn't looking forward to climbing down into the deadly sewers, but at least it would get him away from these two foul-mouthed raccoons.

"Look, Kit *is* scared," Flynn said. "Oh dear. Well, now he'll be eaten for sure."

"Serves him right for what he did to us," said Shane. "And we, who merely tried to play a friendly game of chance."

"Like Ma used to say," added Flynn, "in a game of luck, you test your pluck, but in a game of chance—"

"You can lose your pants!" Shane finished the rhyme.

Kit did his best to ignore the jabbering brothers the rest of the way to the sewer grate. It was an unassuming hole in the ground. Bits of trash and leaves had clumped up over the entrance, and Kit had to pull the filthy mess away with his paws, while the Blacktail brothers watched.

When Kit had cleared the opening enough to squeeze inside, he took off his hat and set it beside the hole. He didn't want to lose it down in the sewer.

"If I don't make it back, could you give that to Eeni?" he asked.

Shane Blacktail leaned down over him. "We'll sell your hat to the birds to decorate their nests."

"You guys really are jerks," Kit said, and lowered himself halfway into the hole.

"Tell Gayle to save your head," Flynn snarled. "We'd love to hang it on our wall!"

"It *would* look lovely on our wall," Shane added.

"I just *said* we'd love to hang it on our wall," Shane told him. "Why'd you have to repeat that?"

While the brothers bickered, Kit lowered himself the rest of the way through the hole and let himself drop deep down into the murky water to face whatever dangers lurked below the surface.

The sewer was cool and dark, and the gentle moonlight was far, far above. Kit's nose worked the stale air, which smelled of rainwater, ammonia, old lettuce boiled in sweat socks, and the rotting waste of a million souls up above. It might have turned some creatures' stomachs, but it wasn't an unpleasant smell for a raccoon who loved garbage casserole.

Still, Kit's fur prickled with fear. Through the stinky fog of sewage, he couldn't smell if some giant reptile was smelling him too.

Kit paddled himself over to the edge of the slow-moving stream of sewer water and climbed onto the stone side. Pipes and waste lines crisscrossed one another like a spider's web overhead, carrying water to and from the People's homes. The People had no idea that below them a small raccoon in a patchwork jacket held the fate of the city's wilds in his tiny black paws.

Kit shook out his fur and wrung out his hands. The underground river was cluttered with leaves and sludge, great tangles of plastic bags, and other bits of garbage. As he crawled along beside it, he found himself scampering around even more refuse, huge piles of it. There were broken toys and plastic trays and more balls than he could count. As he walked, he knocked a soccer ball into the river, where it made a splash that sounded to Kit like a clap of thunder.

He froze, fearing that even the smallest noise would alert the alligator to his presence. He watched as the ball bobbed on the surface, drifted a moment, then got hopelessly tangled in a mass of plastic bags and hung forlornly against the opposite bank of the artificial river. The bags, Kit realized, could be just as dangerous as any metal trap. He would have to be careful not to get tangled in them himself. That'd make him easy pickings for an alligator.

Kit started to walk in one direction, began to doubt himself, and turned another way. His ears swiveled, trying to make out a stray splash or misplaced ripple in the water, even though he knew that by the time he heard the alligator's attack it would be too late.

Kit stopped and tapped his fingers on the wall, wondering how he would find one particular spot down here in the huge network of tunnels. Suddenly, his fingers stopped and he looked up. The entire wall was covered in colorful graffiti. The wall opposite too.

He pulled the small stone from his pocket and held it up against the wall. The colors didn't match. This wasn't the right place, but now he knew what to look for. There would be a missing spot in one of the graffiti murals where the Footprint of Azban had broken off.

He started to run along the river, holding up the stone as he ran, comparing it with the swoops and swirls left by countless seasons of young artists who'd braved the sewers before him. The farther he ran, the more despondent he became. None of the artwork seemed to match the shard of stone he had. He saw faces and colors and scenes and words, but not a single paw print. He thought about Azban's riddle: *too low to dig and too high to reach, caged with iron light and locked in threes* and was no closer to understanding it. He knew he'd never find the place by himself.

Well, he thought, there must be one animal down here who knows every swoosh and curl of paint in this place; he just had to figure out how to get the creature to help him instead of eating him.

He took a deep breath and then he whistled. When nothing happened, he sang a song as loud as he could: *"Loo-loo-loon, I'm a juicy plump raccoon; lo-lo-lone, in the sewers all alone."*

He stopped singing and listened. He heard the gentle trickle of the river, the *drip-drip-drip* from the pipes, and the constant rustle of plastic tangling in the current. His keen eyes saw only the river and the garbage floating by on its surface. Except one strange piece of garbage wasn't floating by. Even as the river moved, it stayed put.

It was brown and knotty, like a branch broken off an oak tree.

Except there were no oak trees down in the sewers for a branch to break off from, and tree branches didn't usually have two yellow eyes, blinking in the dark.

"I see that you see me," the alligator spoke, popping her head above the water. Her voice was as deep as the sewer itself, and flowed as smoothly as the water around her. "If you try to run, or move so much as a hair on your tail, I'll swallow you where you stand." Her long snout broke into a toothy grin. "Now tell me, raccoon, who are you and what are you doing down here?"

"I . . . I'm Kit," Kit said. "And I wanted to find you."

"To find me?" The alligator gasped. "No one ever *wants* to find me. In fact, when someone does find me, I am the last thing they ever find. Don't you know that? I am Death and Destruction and Despair!"

The alligator reared back her head, bursting her giant body from the water and opening her mouth so wide that Kit could have stood on his tiptoes on the alligator's tongue, stretched out his paws, and still not touched the roof of her mouth.

"I thought your name was Gayle."

"Yes, well, it is. I am Gayle, but I am also . . ." She cleared her throat and yelled so loud the water rippled around her, "Death and Destruction and Despair!"

"Okay," Kit said, trying to act unimpressed. "Can I just call you Gayle, though? It's much easier."

"You can call me whatever you want," said Gayle. "You won't call me it for long."

"I won't? Why not?"

"Because I am going to eat you!"

"Me? You're going to eat me?" Kit pointed at himself with his paw. "But I'm not much of a meal."

"You'll be a snack."

"I'd rather not."

"Too bad for you!" She lunged at Kit, her jaw slamming shut as she flung herself from the water. Kit dove to the side, and Gayle's jaws caught only a wisp of fur from his tail. It stung tearing out, but made the alligator cough.

Kit ran, and Gayle chased him along the stone walk beside the sewer. He turned a corner, and Gayle shot like a bee's stinger back into the water.

She swam with tremendous speed. Overtaking Kit, she jumped out and opened her mouth directly in front of him.

Kit skittered to a stop and turned down the nearest opening, another stream of the sewer, into which the alligator dove again. "You'll never escape, Kit. I'm gonna chew you up, bones and all!"

"Please don't," Kit yelled. "I'd like to keep my bones. In fact, I need to leave here with one more bone than I came in with."

"Others have tried to find the Bone of Contention," Gayle yelled after him. "And I ate them."

Kit ran as fast as his four paws would carry him. He saw that the sewer ran through a set of metal bars just ahead of him. They were wide enough apart that he could fit through them, but close enough together that the alligator couldn't.

He dove through just as Gayle's jaws tried to snatch him from the air. She slammed her scaly snout into hard metal, then lifted her head above water and glared furiously at Kit.

"Coward," she said. "You come out here and get eaten."

Kit looked back over his shoulder to the tunnel behind him. He could run, but then he'd never find what he was after.

"Listen," said Kit. "We have a problem. We each have

something the other one wants. You want to eat me, and I want to see the painting this came from." He held up the stone with the Footprint of Azban for her to see.

"You're an art lover?" Gayle considered it a moment.

"Sure . . . ," said Kit.

"I am something of an art aficionado myself, you know?" Gayle said. "The walls of this sewer are the finest collection of so-called graffiti in the world. No one ever comes to appreciate my collection, though."

"Well, uh . . . don't you eat them before they get a chance?"

"Sometimes I eat them after," she said. "You think that's why they stopped coming?"

"I think so," said Kit. "So you know where the rest of this painting is?"

"Of course," said Gayle. "But why should I show you?"

"Well, you can't eat me while I'm on the other side of these bars, and I can't find this painting without your help. Why don't we negotiate?"

"If I show you the painting, can I eat you afterward?" Gayle suggested.

Kit smirked, because he had her now. She was stronger than he was, but he was cleverer and—thanks to the Blacktail brothers—now Kit knew that no one in Ankle Snap Alley played fair. He didn't have to, and couldn't expect that Gayle would either.

"Well, sure," said Kit. "That seems like an even trade. *If* you can chew me. I don't want to be swallowed whole."

"Of course I can chew you!" said Gayle. "Look at my teeth! They can chew a hundred raccoons! A thousand!"

"I dunno," said Kit. "Your teeth don't look so strong. Maybe this negotiation won't work."

"My teeth *are* strong," said the alligator. "Come out here and find out how very strong they are."

The alligator thrashed her tail wildly, splashing water this way and that. She roared and snapped her powerful jaws so hard the breeze off her teeth ruffled Kit's fur. She bit at the metal bars, pulled and tugged, but much to Kit's relief, the bars held.

"See?" said Kit. "How could you bite through a raccoon with those weak teeth? I bet you couldn't even bite through a plastic bag."

"I could too," said the alligator.

"Prove it," said Kit. "If you can bite through that plastic bag behind you, then I'll come out and you can bite through me too, after you take me to the painting where the Footprint of Azban came from."

The alligator thought a moment. There was a devious twinkle in her yellow eyes, and she blinked sideways twice while she thought. "I accept," the alligator said.

Chapter Twenty-One

LOST AND FOUND

OKAY, said Kit. He stretched so that Gayle could get a mouthwatering look at his belly. He could see the hunger in her eyes, which was just what Kit wanted. It was hard to think clearly when you were consumed by animal desire. "Try to bite through that plastic bag."

Gayle shook her head from side to side on her giant neck and chuckled. "Foolish boy. This bet will be the last you ever make." She flung herself into the water and vanished below the surface. All was still. All was quiet.

A moment later, the alligator burst from the water,

flashing her scales, gnashing her teeth, and tearing the bundle of plastic bags to bits.

"Thee? Ha-ha!" the alligator cried out, victorious. "I'fe goth them thorn thoo threds . . . wait . . . why am I thalking like thith?"

She shook her head, her tiny claws trying to grab the bits of plastic from out of her teeth, but her arms were too short and the plastic too tangled. The alligator's tongue flailed around, trying to pick free all the shredded bits of bags, but the more she struggled, the more tangled she became.

"Outh! Now my thongue ith thangled!" the alligator cried out. She'd managed to knot the bits of plastic around her tongue and three of her teeth, and the more she wriggled, the worse it got. After a few minutes of flopping and flailing and yelling and wailing, the alligator slumped sadly on stones beside the water, just on the opposite side of the bars from Kit. She groaned.

"You okay, Gayle?" Kit asked, his voice as sympathetic as he could make it sound.

"Mrmm mrmmm mrrmmm," the alligator responded. She'd become so tangled in plastic that she couldn't even open her mouth. She snorted a blast of hot air through her nostrils and blinked at Kit sadly. She was as caught up in self-pity as she was in plastic.

"You're all stuck," said Kit. "I guess I could help you."

The alligator nodded, then opened her eyes wide again, whimpering. But Kit didn't trust her.

"Well, I won our bet, so why don't you honor *that* first," said Kit, sliding out from between the bars to stand beside the dejected reptile. "Show me the painting and then I'll untie your jaws."

The alligator nodded glumly, then plodded off along the stones, her tail dragging in somber zigzags behind her. She didn't jump back into the water, and Kit padded along next to her, keeping an eye on her mouth in case she got her jaws free on her own.

"Don't feel too bad," said Kit. "All this is for a good cause. If I can find the Bone of Contention, I can show the Flealess that we wild animals have a right to live where we please."

Gayle blinked, which Kit guessed meant she understood. They walked down a long sewer tunnel and stopped in front of a brick archway where the water didn't flow. Gayle went through the arch first and Kit followed.

They stood side by side in a cavernous space that looked like it had once been a train station, but had been empty for a long time. They stood on a platform over long-abandoned train tracks. Above them hung three old chandeliers, draped in cobwebs so thick their original shapes couldn't even be seen. Moonlight streaked in from the metal grates overhead, and there was a vast mural painted all over the walls, colorful swoops and swirls in the styles of a hundred different artists. Kit held the stone up and, sure enough, saw the same color and shape along the far wall. He rushed over to it and found the spot where a piece of the wall was missing, just at raccoon height.

He pressed the stone into the blank space and held his paw there against the paw print of Azban. This was the place his mother and father had been searching for. He felt history connecting him to his parents and, through his parents, to the First Raccoon and to all of raccoonkind.

"This is it, Ma," he whispered. "I found it."

"Dis inn irt," Gayle muttered through her plastic-muzzled jaw. "Et eee oooot."

He didn't let Gayle out just yet. He traced the Footprint of Azban along the wall and saw, almost completely painted over in hot pink spray paint, another footprint, and another after that, much older than the paint that covered them.

He followed the paw prints on the wall around and up and down and side to side, scurrying in the path of his long-lost ancestor, until the path stopped at a mural that didn't look like the other graffiti on the wall. The colors were faded browns and reds and greens, more like the colors an animal might paint with than a Person. The image was crude, but it looked like the painting of a dog and a raccoon and a mouse from the pamphlet Kit had seen, except done in stick figures, surrounded by tiny mouse paw prints and big dog paw prints and the same elegant raccoon paw prints he'd followed to get here. They were playing the shell-and-nut game. Brutus was frowning and Azban was laughing and the mouse scribes were swinging from the chandeliers.

"This is where Azban hid the Bone," Kit declared.

He tapped the wall, but it felt solid. He looked down at his feet, but the ground, too, was solid. He couldn't imagine where the Bone could be hidden.

Too low to dig and too high to reach, caged with iron light and locked in threes.

He broke the riddle down into its parts.

"Too low to dig," he wondered aloud. Gayle grunted something. "That's it!" Kit said. "We're too low in the sewers for anyone to dig down here. Then he pointed up at the chandeliers. "And they're too high to reach even for a hundred raccoons standing on one another's shoulders . . . and made of iron, like the one in this drawing." He tapped the wall. "They give off light. Iron light!"

"Mmm ocked nnn eeees?" Gayle said, which Kit figured was her asking what he was thinking: *What did it mean, "locked in threes"?*

There were three chandeliers, so maybe the Bone was hidden in one of them . . . like the shell-and-nut game. He had to guess which of the three.

It couldn't be that simple, though. The Rat King said

Azban liked tricks, and he knew from experience that the shell-and-nut game was designed for trickery. He decided to do a test. He picked up a broken piece of tile from the floor, felt its weight in his hand, and then tossed it at the nearest chandelier.

The tile sailed through the cobwebs and hit the metal on the other side with a clunk. For an instant, nothing happened.

And then, the chain that held the iron chandelier to the ceiling creaked, rumbled, and retracted, zipping up into itself and snapping the iron candelabra prongs of the chandelier shut like a trap.

Tile dust rained down. The tile had been pulverized, and had he been up there looking for the Bone, he'd have been pulverized too.

"I guess that isn't the one," said Kit. "It's gotta be hidden in one of the other two. Guess I'll use the process of elimination."

He picked up another piece of tile and flung it at the second chandelier.

Nothing happened.

He picked up one more broken piece and threw it at the third chandelier. Nothing happened to that one either.

No help there. The trap for the other wrong choice must be different. It could be anything, spikes or blades or poison. He'd only get one chance to choose, and if he chose wrong, it'd probably kill him.

He walked around beneath them both, looking up, considering. He needed a hint. He needed some clue about which chandelier was the right chandelier and which chandelier was a death trap.

He studied the drawing again. Brutus was pointing at an empty shell and Azban was laughing. That's when Kit noticed a nut tucked into the raccoon's paw, wedged in the spot between his thumb and forefinger, sleight of paw.

Kit thought about the shell game he'd played with the Blacktail brothers. He'd been so sure about which shell hid the nut because he was right. But as soon as he chose, Shane was able to sneak it out from that shell and slide it under a different one. At the moment he'd won, he'd lost. The nut wasn't under any of the shells—it was in the raccoon's hand.

He looked back up at the chandeliers. And beyond them, all the way at the top of the ceiling, was the grate that let in the moonlight. The grate was iron, like a cage! The chandeliers were a trick. The Bone was hidden in the grate!

But how was he supposed to get up there?

He looked back at Gayle, still all tangled up in plastic and looking pretty glum about it.

"I need you to fling me," Kit said. She cocked her head

at him. "I'm going to stand on your tail, and you can fling me up to that grate. I'll tie the plastic to my ankle, and that way, when I go flying off you, the bags'll come off too."

She looked doubtful, but nodded. What choice did she have?

Kit got to work on the plastic, loosening it in just the right places, tying an end around his own foot. Once he was ready, he nodded to Gayle, climbed onto her tail, and gave a shout.

"Whoop!" he said, and Gayle flung him, the force of her tail sending him all the way to the ceiling. The plastic around his ankle pulled tight, but the plastic around her snout and in her teeth unspooled as he flew and set Gayle free.

But she hadn't flung him far enough. He was headed straight for a chandelier. If he didn't catch on, he'd plummet to the hard concrete below. If he did catch on, he could spring a trap that'd crush him.

He heard Eeni's voice in his head: *You walk out the door, and you never know what'll happen next.*

She had that right.

He stretched his arms wide and caught the chandelier in a great hug that sent it swinging. His snout filled with cobwebs. And then he heard the sound of the chain unraveling. The chandelier was rigged to fall.

One look down, and he saw Gayle, waiting below him with her mouth open wide.

He thrust with his back legs, springing from the iron light fixture to the next one, catching on with his front paws and swinging himself up. The first chandelier smashed to bits on the concrete. He had no time to rest, because his weight had sprung the second trap too. A trickle of oil flowed down the chain and filled narrow channels in each arm of the chandelier, including the one he was holding. Then there was a spark and the oil burst into flames.

"Ah!" Kit yelled, kicking his legs to make the whole flaming contraption swing. The fur on his paws singed and his bare black palms burned, but he heaved and swung and kicked free like a flying squirrel and flew the long leap toward the moonlight.

He caught his fingers between the metal grate and pulled himself up. On the other side of the bars, he saw a big bone lying on its side, and he could make out the footprints of three animals inked onto it: the mouse, the dog, and the raccoon.

He'd found the Bone of Contention, just like he'd promised his mother he would. He stretched his little paw through and gripped it. It slid out perfectly between the bars. A creature with bigger paws wouldn't have been able to get it and a smaller creature won't have been able to make the jump he'd made. It was hidden in the perfect location for a raccoon.

"Thanks, Azban," Kit whispered to the moonlight,

clutching the bone to his chest. Now he just had to get back to the Rabid Rascals with it . . . and not get eaten in the process.

He looked all the way down at the alligator circling below. Her jaws snapped open and shut loudly. The flaming chandelier made her a giant dancer against the graffitied wall.

"Okay," she said. "You got your bone! Now I'm hungry!"

Kit had to think of something tastier to offer her than himself.

"Hey, Gayle," Kit called. "How about we make another deal?"

The alligator stopped circling and waited.

That's when Kit suggested something brand-new. The alligator licked her lips as she listened to Kit's proposal.

Chapter Twenty-Two
DEAL BREAKER

HERE'S one," Shane Blacktail told his brother, with a grin on his face. "How many raccoons does it take to find the Bone of Contention?"

"I don't know, brother. How many?" Flynn Blacktail responded.

"No one knows!" Shane cheered, delivering the gleeful punch line to his joke. "They all get eaten when they try."

The Blacktail brothers doubled over laughing, but Eeni and Uncle Rik did not find the joke funny at all. They were locked in separate cages that had been hoisted up by pulleys to the van's ceiling so that they hung above the dashboard, visible to all the thugs and goons of the Rabid Rascals and to the passersby outside in Ankle Snap Alley.

Uncle Rik watched sadly as a family of rabbits lifted their meager belongings onto their backs and made their way out of the alley. The green tops of carrots poked from their satchels. Five young hedgehogs followed them, along with a scurry of baby squirrels from the Asylum for Bush-Tailed Orphans. There were a teenaged ferret and a newborn mole in the group too. The church mice who ran the orphans' asylum scurried after the children, trying to keep them together as they made their way into exile from Ankle Snap Alley.

"Can't you see what's happening?" Uncle Rik called down to the turtle. "Everyone is leaving. They think the Flealess are going to evict them."

"The seven hundred and seven seasons are over," the Turtle said without even lifting his head from inside his shell. "What do you want me to do about it?"

"Let us help Kit," Eeni cried out. "If we can find the Bone of Contention, we can prove we belong here."

The turtle's eyes glistened in the shadow of his shell. "A bet's a bet. If Kit can find the Bone himself, then we'll see what we can do about the Flealess. If he can't . . . well . . ."

Rik looked at the porcupine below. He was puffing out and relaxing his quills over and over again, testing them for sharpness. Rik shuddered and glanced at the door, hoping Kit would return, but also fearful that if he did, the turtle would still have them all tortured just for spite. He didn't stay the boss of the Rabid Rascals by losing bets with young raccoons.

Blue Neck Ned, still upset he'd been kicked out of his table at Ansel's bakery, had perched on the gearshift, and he watched Eeni and Rik like a hawk . . . well, more like an angry pigeon with a grudge.

"Bet you wish you hadn't taken my seat now, don't ya, Rik?" Blue Neck Ned mocked Kit's uncle.

"I feel so helpless stuck in here." Eeni rattled her cage. "If Kit were here, he could break us out."

Rik shook his head. "I could break us out too, young lady. Any raccoon worth the stripes on his tail can pick a lock, but it wouldn't do much good. I don't think either of us can fight off a pack of mangy dogs, a murderous porcupine, and a python."

Basil snored quietly coiled in a corner, but he smirked to show he heard them talking about him.

"You forgot pigeon," Blue Neck Ned added. "You'd have to fight me off too."

"That wouldn't be a problem," said Rik, locking eyes with the bird.

"Why you no-good, down-and-out, garbage-scrounging liar." The pigeon ruffled his feathers. "I don't need to wait for Kit. That boy ain't coming back! Now I'm going to show you what happens when you mess with *this* pigeon."

The bird leaped from the gearshift onto the top of the cage and started pecking down through the bars at Rik's ears.

"Ow, stop that," Rik shouted. "Get off of me!" He punched up with his claws, but Ned danced from side to side as he pecked, shaking the cage and knocking Rik off his feet.

"Cut it out up there, youse!" The boss popped his head out of his shell. "A turtle can't hardly think with all that noise."

"He's giving me guff," Blue Neck Ned said. "He's gotta learn to respect a bird like me."

"Respect is earned," the old turtle said. "And a bird like you hasn't earned it from anyone."

Ned's wings flexed, but he didn't reply. A pigeon who talked back to the boss turtle could get his wings clipped faster than a mosquito fries on a bug zapper.

"We will wait until the boy returns or the sun comes up and the bet is lost," the turtle said. "Until then, Rik and his young rat friend are our guests. And we do not *peck* at our guests."

"You think the boy will come back to give up the Bone, Bossss?" Basil asked.

The turtle shrugged. "No, I don't think he'll come back to give up the Bone." He looked at Rik and smiled.

"I don't think he'll come back at all. Even if he finds it, there's Gayle, who wouldn't let a tasty morsel like him out of her sewer alive."

Just then, the van door slid open with a startling crash.

"You're wrong, Turtle!" Kit declared. The sky had just begun to swell with morning light, and his fur was tinted red against the glow. The dogs circled, sniffing the wet fur and sewage smell that clung to him. "She's a very reasonable reptile." He held up the Bone. "And I win."

"How . . . how did you get away from her?" Shane stammered.

"We made a deal," said Kit.

"What kind of a deal?" The turtle narrowed his eyes suspiciously.

"That's between me and Gayle," said Kit. "Now let my friends go."

The turtle nodded. "Well played, Kit, well played indeed!" The turtle gestured to Shane and Flynn. "Let 'em out."

"But, Boss!" Shane and Flynn objected together.

"A deal's a deal," said the Turtle. "We Rascals pay what's owed."

Kit glowered at Shane and Flynn as they let Eeni, Martyn, and Uncle Rik out of their cages. "I want my hat back too."

Flynn grumbled, but pulled it out of the glove compartment and tossed it to Kit.

Uncle Rik touched his paw to the image of Azban's paw

inscribed on the Bone that Kit held. "You really found it," he said. His eyes filled with wonder. "Your parents would be so proud."

Kit smiled.

"We can show this to the Flealess," said Martyn. "We can show them we have the right to live here for good."

"Well, it's not up to us," said Kit. "A deal's a deal."

He tossed the Bone into the sand in front of the turtle.

"You can't give him that!" Martyn protested.

"I may not be able to make everyone else around here keep their promises, but I can sure as seasons keep mine," said Kit. He looked back to his uncle. "Still think Mom and Dad would be proud of me?"

"I know they would," said Uncle Rik. "You're a raccoon of your word, brave and quick of paw. What more could they hope for?"

"A raccoon who doesn't give priceless artifacts away to gangsters?" Kit suggested.

"Hey," said the turtle. "We live here too, you know. What good's running a neighborhood if the Flealess think they can kick us out? This Bone says we get to stay, and that's what we're gonna do."

Kit's uncle hugged him. "See?" he said. "You did well. Now I think we ought to go back to my apartment and get some well-deserved rest. Eeni, I'm sure your own family is wondering where you've gotten off to."

"Uh, right, sure . . . ," said Eeni.

"You do have somewhere to go, don't you, Eeni?" Kit asked.

"Of course I do!" Eeni snapped back at him. "I spend most nights with some squirrels in the old theater."

"The dancing squirrels?" Uncle Rik shook his head. "That's no place for a young rat like yourself."

Eeni shrugged. "I do just fine," she said.

"By my stripes you do!" Uncle Rik said. "You'll stay with us tonight. I've a comfy couch you can sleep on and a newspaper quilt that's cozy as can be."

Kit noticed Eeni looked bashful, like she might turn down the offer out of pride. Since he'd arrived in the alley, he'd heard all kinds of creatures lie for all kinds of bad reasons, so he decided he could tell a lie for a good reason.

"Oh, please stay with us," he said. "You're my only friend in this city, and I'll be so lonely without you."

After he said it, he realized it wasn't quite a lie after all.

"Okay," Eeni agreed. "I'll come along . . . for your sake."

She looked relieved.

Just then, Basil cleared his throat. "Exsssscusssse me, Bossss," the snake said. "I have sssome bad newsssss."

"What is it, Basil?" the turtle grunted.

"I've taken a new job, sssseee?" Basil smiled. "My new employer offered me a very comfortable exsssissstencccce in the houssssessss."

"In the houses?" The turtle narrowed his eyes at his enforcer. "You mean the Flealess?"

"I do," said Basil. "And my firsssst job for them issss thisssss."

Without another word, Basil struck at the sand in front of the pool.

The turtle's head retreated into his shell. Blue Neck Ned screeched and took off in a panicked flight, slamming right into the windshield and knocking himself out. Shane and Flynn screamed and tried to shove themselves into the glove compartment as Basil swallowed the Bone of Contention whole and spun around to face Kit.

The bone-shaped outline in his neck slid slowly down his gullet. He couldn't speak, but he gave Kit a wink and a nod of thanks, then rushed from the van, zigging and zagging into the alley.

"Hey!" shouted Martyn, waving his fist. "You can't steal that!"

The brave little mouse chased after the snake, while Eeni, Kit, and Rik stood dumbfounded. The Rabid Rascals had just been cheated, and now the Bone was lost and, with it, any claim the Wild Ones had to call Ankle Snap Alley their home.

Part IV

THE BATTLE FOR ANKLE SNAP ALLEY

Chapter Twenty-Three

THE DOG'S DAY

SIXCLAW licked his orange paw as he waited for the tiny dog to prance across the sidewalk to him. The People had all left their homes for the day. The neighborhood belonged to the Flealess now.

The sun glinted off the bell around the orange cat's neck, which dinged every time he smoothed the fur behind his ears. He had trained the whole neighborhood to quake at the sound of his bell. He often didn't need to do anything more than make it chime to get a creature to confess their deepest secrets to him.

Of course, he liked it more when they resisted. Then he got to use his claws.

"So you got the snake to turn on his own kind?" Sixclaw asked Titus.

"I got the snake to remember where he came from," Titus said. "He began as a well-fed house pet, and I promised him he could return to being one. In exchange for the Bone."

"Reptiles," Sixclaw grunted. "Can't trust 'em."

"He did what you could not," said the dog. "He retrieved the Bone."

"Funny, I thought only dogs played fetch."

"Don't you dare insult me, you bird-breathed doorknob scratcher!" Titus barked.

He loathed these cats and their pride. They ate the People's food, drank their water, and accepted their care, but still, they thought they were somehow better than the other Flealess, just because they lived outside. As far as Titus was concerned, Sixclaw was little better than the wild vermin he so hated. He was no house cat. For all Titus knew, Sixclaw actually did have fleas.

"You know, Basil brought me a present too," Sixclaw said. He produced a small sack he'd tucked into his collar and untied the drawstring. He dropped the pouch on the ground with a thump, and a small mouse rolled out, his white robes dirty and torn. The little rodent squinted up at the sudden sunlight. "Hello, Martyn," Sixclaw said.

Martyn looked up at the looming faces of the cat and the dog. "You shampoo-stinking monsters," he yelled. "The Bone of Contention *does* give us the right to stay, and you know it! It's proof that your ancestor did make a deal with Azban. You can't hide from the truth."

Titus circled the mouse on the ground. "I have had enough of ancient history, you sanctimonious cheese eater! Who cares what deal was made so long ago? We're not historians, we're animals. Our way is tooth and claw; our law is power. We don't bark and bargain for our turf. We take it! Now that I've got your precious proof, I'm going to bury it so deep, not even your ghost will be able to find it."

"So you're going to pretend like it never existed?" Martyn asked.

"He who controls history, controls the future," said Titus. "Without it, the vermin have no claim to call this alley home."

"You are the dirtiest, stinkingest, lyingest, bedbug-brained canine I have ever—"

Before Martyn could finish, Sixclaw swooped him back up in the sack and cinched it shut. The mouse's voice shouted on, muffled to nonsense by the fabric.

"A useful little prize," Titus told the cat.

"I was going to eat him," said Sixclaw.

"First, I want you to send an eviction notice to the vermin. Tell them they are to leave their homes and shops immediately or be destroyed. The alley is ours, and anyone left in it when the sun reaches its peak is pet food."

"The sun's already up," the cat observed. "The vermin will be sleeping."

"So?" The dog shook his head. "Wake them. I'm sure Martyn's friends can be of help in that."

The cat smiled. "So it's war then?"

"War?" The dog sat back and scratched his ear. "No. Not war. This, I think, will be a massacre. You'll bring the outdoor cats?"

"Of course," said Sixclaw. "On one condition."

"What's that?"

"When this is done, I get to eat Kit's head," the cat said.

"You and your heads." The dog scratched behind his ear. "Fine. You may eat his head."

Sixclaw licked his lips.

Titus thought the feline assassin could use a visit to the veterinarian to treat his obsession with eating heads, but the dog had bigger things to worry about than one crazy killer cat. His parents always told him that some dogs were bred to greatness, some were given greatness by their People, and some, like him, had to grab greatness by the scruff of its neck and tear it to pieces for themselves.

He could taste the greatness on the tip of his tongue.

Or maybe that was toilet water.

Either way, it was going to be a delicious day.

It was time to lead the Flealess to battle.

Chapter Twenty-Four

PAMPHLETEERS

KIT and Eeni helped Uncle Rik hang a new front door, shared a snail-and-Snickers sandwich from Ansel's bakery, and lay down, dejected, to get some rest.

Kit curled into a ball on Uncle Rik's sofa, and Eeni curled into a ball on his tail. Uncle Rik laid the newspaper quilt over them both.

"So . . . what now?" Kit asked. "They took the Bone."

His uncle sighed. "I don't know, Kit. I just don't know."

"Do you think they'll kick us out of the alley?"

Uncle Rik nodded. "I do. But I don't want you to worry about it. You've done enough worrying for a raccoon your age. When the time comes, we'll find a new home somewhere, I promise. Now get some sleep."

Just before closing the shade to block out the sun, Uncle Rik cleared his throat, getting both the young animals' attention one more time.

"I have to ask, Kit," Uncle Rik said. "What kind of a deal did you make with the alligator to escape her sewer?"

"You really want to know?" Kit asked. Uncle Rik nodded. "I promised her a better snack than me . . . I promised her the six-clawed cat who killed my parents."

Uncle Rik gasped. "I am not comfortable with this bargain."

"I had to offer her *something*, or I never would have made it back to rescue you," Kit explained.

"But this promise to her . . ." Uncle Rik shook his head. "It's too terrible to think about. You aren't a killer."

"I'm not going to kill anybody," Kit protested.

"You may not be the jaws snapping shut on that cat," said Uncle Rik. "But if you put the cat on the menu, then you are responsible for it."

Kit looked down at his paws. He blushed. "Well, it's not like I can just hand over the cat to Gayle anyway. I don't have a dinner bell to ring for a sewer alligator."

"It's a good thing you don't," said Uncle Rik. "There is no shame in feeling angry at what Sixclaw did to your family, but Wild Ones do not seek revenge. It is not our way.

The Flealess and their so-called civilization hold grudges and seek vengeance, but in the wild, we forgive and we forget. It is the only way to survive."

"You want me to forget my parents?" Kit growled.

"No," said Uncle Rik. "I want their memory to be a source of joy, not anger. Celebrate the time you had with them, not the way they were stolen from you. Choosing what our memories make us is the privilege we have as intelligent animals. If you want to spend your life remembering everyone who wrongs you, you can, but wouldn't you rather be a source of goodness in the world?"

Kit studied his paw and thought. He looked at Eeni. "It's kinda like what you say down here, isn't it? We're born with a howl and go out with a snap, but it's what we do in between that matters."

"Howl to snap," Eeni agreed.

"Howl to snap," said Kit.

"Howl to snap," said Uncle Rik.

Kit smiled and closed his eyes. He could feel Eeni's breath rising and falling where she rested on his tail. He was amazed at how quickly she fell asleep. He figured when you lived on the mean streets of Ankle Snap Alley, you learned to steal whatever sleep you could get as fast as you could get it.

Before he knew it, he was asleep too. He dreamed he saw his mother and father sitting around a table, playing the shell-and-nut game with Azban, who was sweeping his winnings off the table into the mouth of an alligator.

"But I picked the right shell," his mother cried out. "I win."

"No such thing as winning in shells-and-nuts," said Azban with a wink. "I should know. I invented the game."

"But I found the nut. You can't just change the rules of a game as you go along." His father stood from the table.

Azban turned to look at Kit, who was suddenly standing in front of the table, dressed like a warrior in armor. The old raccoon spoke not in one voice, but in a hundred voices, like the Rat King had. "Who says we are playing a game?"

BANG! BANG! BANG!

A loud knocking at the door dissolved the dream and snapped Kit awake. Eeni was already standing, pulling on her vest. Uncle Rik came scurrying down the hall.

"Who is it?" he shouted. "Who's knocking on my door in the middle of the day? Don't they know we're trying to sleep?"

On flinging the door open, Uncle Rik saw a crowd of church mice trembling in their white robes. The one in front had a black eye and a bruise on his head. The other church mice didn't look much better off.

"They . . . they . . . they just . . . ," the mouse said.

"Say it, mouse!" Uncle Rik bellowed. "Why are you

knocking at my door at this unmousely hour? What's happened?"

The mouse thrust out his paw, holding a crudely printed pamphlet, which Uncle Rik took from him. "That cat . . . ," the harried mouse said through trembling snout. "He burst into our print shop just as we were getting ready for bed. He took us by surprise . . . He threatened to eat Martyn if we didn't print this out and give it to everyone in the alley."

Uncle Rik looked up and down the alley and saw all the groggy creatures roused from slumber, terrified mice at their doors handing them pamphlets. Enrique Gallo, the rooster, stood in the doorway to his barbershop with a sleeping mask hanging from his beak. His feathers ruffled as he read the pamphlet in his talon.

Ansel and Otis stood in the doorway to their home beside the bakery, wearing matching pajamas and matching frowns, reading what the mice had given them.

Even the news finches were silent as they read, and the Rabid Rascals had gone to wake the turtle with a pamphlet.

"We had no choice . . . ," the mouse muttered. "The Flealess have Martyn. We had to do as they said. I'm sorry, Kit. We had to . . ."

Uncle Rik looked at the pamphlet in his paws. Eeni and Kit had come up behind him to read over his shoulder.

SWORN TESTIMONY OF MARTYN, CHIEF SCRIBE OF CHURCH MICE

Made on this morning of the 707th Season

As Chief Scribe and Keeper of History, I, Martyn, Parish Scribe, swear before these witnesses that there is no such object as THE BONE OF CONTENTION, nor has there ever been a DEAL giving rights and privileges to the VERMIN of Ankle Snap Alley. All claims by one juvenile Raccoon calling himself "Kit" are false. We are SADDENED that one so young could be so CORRUPT, and we URGE all creatures of the alley to DISFAVOR, DISREGARD, AND DISOWN said raccoon and his family now and for all time.

Pack your things! Leave Ankle Snap Alley! The Seven Hundred Seven Seasons have ended, and this turf belongs to the FLEALESS at mid-sun today.

SAVE YOURSELVES and GO!

Sworn & Sealed,
Martyn H. Musculus, Church Mouse

Kit could feel all eyes in the alley turn to look in his direction. Every creature was sizing him up, trying to decide what to do with him. In a place full of liars, cheats, and thieves, he had just become the worst of the lot. To them he'd done something worse than cheat. He'd given them hope, then taken it away. That was about the most terrible thing one fellow could do to another.

"The Bone's real!" he protested. "It's that letter there that's fake!" He jabbed his paw at the pamphlet. "Martyn would never use the word *vermin* to describe us! Can't you see? They're just trying to scare you. The Flealess want you all to give up and leave the alley without a fight!" He pleaded with the mice. "Tell them the truth," he begged. "Tell them this is a lie!"

"I'm so sorry," the mouse whispered. "They have Martyn." Then he shouted so all the alley could hear. "This is the truth. We don't have the Bone; we cannot prove otherwise!" He whispered again to Kit, "So sorry."

But whispered apologies aren't worth the air they're whispered with, and the damage of the lie was done.

The alley turned on Kit.

Chapter Twenty-Five

HOME IS WHERE THE FIGHT IS

ALL the animals stepped from their doorways and moved toward Uncle Rik's apartment. Their morning shadows stretched in Kit's direction, as if a hundred shadow claws already had him in their grasp. The largest shadow of all loomed toward him, and he saw it was cast by the rooster, Enrique, who strutted across the alley giving Kit a pitiless side-eye.

Eeni stepped in front of Kit in the doorway. She flashed him a frightened smile. "Howl to snap," she said, then shouted at the big rooster and the pack of animals forming behind him. "You leave Kit alone," she shouted. "He's the only honest fellow I've ever met. I saw the Bone with my own eyes."

"Then you're a liar too," shouted a hedgehog in a dirty bowler hat. He'd already packed his belongings into a sack tied to the end of a stick. "Put them on the train tracks," he yelled. "All liars tied to the tracks!"

The other alley animals surged forward behind Enrique the rooster.

"*You're* all liars," yelled Enrique Gallo, raising his sharp talons in the air, and the crowd behind him fell silent. He leaned down to face Kit. "This paper says, however, that you lied about something very important to us, young one," the rooster told him. "What do you say, Kit?"

Kit swallowed. His throat was dry and his voice cracked when he spoke. "I . . . uh . . . *didn't*?"

Enrique sighed. He whispered to Kit. "You have to do better than that, boy. These creatures are scared, and they need to believe in something. Prove it. Prove to us the Bone is real. The Flealess are coming."

"I . . ." Kit looked around. Every animal in the alley hung on his words. The turtle popped his head from the Rabid Rascals' van. "They saw it! The Rascals saw it too."

All eyes turned to the old turtle. He shook his head slowly. "Who can say what I saw?"

"What?!" Kit shouted. "What are you saying? You *did*

see it. Your own snake is the one who stole it."

"I'm sorry, kid," the turtle said. Then he turned to the rest of the Wild Ones. "All who value your lives, pack up and go."

"But you can't say that," Eeni objected. "Everyone paid you for protection."

"What do you want from me?" The turtle shrugged. "They got my snake. I can't protect this place without him."

"Basil sided with the Flealess?" Ansel gasped.

"Oh, that's bad," said Otis. "That's very bad."

"Extra! Extra!" shouted one of the news finches. "Ankle Snap Is Over! Pack Your Nuts and Hit the Struts!"

"No, no," Kit shouted. "We can't just give up."

"We can't prove anything without that Bone," the rooster said. "We gotta go."

He turned away, parting the crowd as he clucked back toward his shop to pack his things.

"Who cares about the Bone?" Kit yelled, and the rooster stopped. The crowd looked back at him. "My parents died so I could find it, and now I'm saying so what? I can't prove I found it, and I can't prove it gives us the right to live here. So. What. No one, not even the Rat King, can really know what happened seven hundred seven seasons ago. But we can know what's happening now!

"The Flealess say this turf is theirs, that our time is

up. We say we have a right to be here. But if we flee at the first sign of trouble, if we turn on one another and lie to one another when our community is threatened, then what right do we have to claim anywhere as our turf? What right do we have to call anywhere home?

"A home isn't made by some deal. It isn't a promise made by history. A home is made by friends who trust one another." He stepped out from behind Eeni, stood proudly in front of the crowd. "It's made by neighbors who share with one another, in good times and bad, even if they don't always get along." He nodded to the Blacktail brothers, then turned to Uncle Rik. "And it's made by family.

"I've lost my home once already," he told the crowd. "And I've lost my family too. But coming here to Ankle Snap Alley, I found a new home, a new family, and I'm not leaving it. So I don't care if some old Bone *says* this is my turf. This is my turf because I'm making it mine; I'm living my life here, and I'm growing up here. If the Flealess don't want to share it, then I'll fight for it here, because I'm a Wild One and my turf is wherever I say it is!"

"I'm with you, Kit," Eeni declared.

The crowd stared back in silence.

Eeni frowned. "Hm, I really thought that would work. Like a cheer or something."

"Well, I'm with you too, Kit," said Uncle Rik. "You're family, and if you're staying, I'm staying."

"Oh, shucks," cried out Possum Ansel. "That Flealess pussycat broke my bakery. The least I can do is get some payback. We're with you too, Kit!"

"We are?" said Otis at his side.

"Yes," said Ansel. "We are."

Otis smiled. "Good. I owe that cat a punch in the jaw."

"If there's a fight with the Flealess coming, then I'm in it too," announced Rocks the dog, who usually slept in front of Larkanon's. He was awake now and standing tall on his four legs.

"Nicely done," said Enrique Gallo, stretching out his rooster wings. "I'm staying too. I've got some fight left in me yet."

"What about you?" Uncle Rik pointed his paw to the rusted old van. All eyes locked on the turtle, waiting for word from the most powerful animal in the alley, whether or not the Rabid Rascals would join the Wild Ones or flee like the Flealess wanted.

The old turtle cleared his throat. "I'd like to be more circumspect about this," said the turtle. "It is no small thing to go into battle against powerful foes."

Kit felt deflated. The Rabid Rascals were the toughest creatures in the alley. It'd be hard to fight off the Flealess without them.

"But," said the turtle, "we will . . . join this fight." He gave Kit a wink. "We're no leash lovers."

"Boss!" Flynn Blacktail complained. "We really gonna risk our necks to help this raccoon after what he done to us?"

"He's a cheat and a liar!" Shane cried out.

"And a liar and a cheat!" Flynn added. Shane glared at him.

"And that is exactly why we'll help him," the old turtle said. "Because he's a cheat and a liar, and he belongs here, with us in Ankle Snap Alley." The turtle gave Kit a respectful nod. "From howl to snap."

"From howl to snap," Kit replied.

"Don't make any mistake," Shane interjected. "When this is over, it all goes back to normal."

"We still run this alley," added Flynn.

"You mean *I* still run this alley," the turtle corrected them both. The twin raccoons blushed for the first time anyone had ever seen.

Kit couldn't help but smile. All the animals around him were hungry-eyed cheats, flea-bitten criminals, and no-good, garbage-scrounging liars . . . but they were a community, *his* community.

"So, Kit," Blue Neck Ned cooed, "you got a plan to fight the Flealess or just a lot of big speeches?"

Kit looked down at his paws, and from one end of the alley to the other. He looked at Eeni and at his uncle Rik and at the big houses of the People where the Flealess lurked, and he thought about his parents and the pack of dogs that hunted them down and the cruel orange cat who ordered them to do it and then he nodded.

"I think I do," he said. "We're going to need garbage. A whole lot of it too. The stinkier, the better."

"Stinky garbage?" Eeni questioned him. "How's that gonna help us beat the Flealess?"

"They think we're all no-good dirty-rotten garbage-scrounging liars," explained Kit. "So we're gonna show 'em just how dirty we can get."

Chapter Twenty-Six

BIRDS OF A FEATHER

THE sun reached its peak at the top of the Slivered Sky. Just as Titus had planned it, there wasn't so much as a shadow off a garbage can for wild vermin to hide in. He stood on point in the alley, one paw raised, nose working the air. His Flealess army amassed around him.

Nothing else moved. The closed sign on Enrique Gallo's Fur Styling Shop and Barbería rattled in a breeze. Leaves brushed against the trash-can lid that shuttered P.

Ansel's bakery. Not even the stray mutt who guarded the door at Larkanon's was to be seen.

Had the vermin really heeded the warnings and abandoned the alley to their betters?

Titus closed his eyes and sniffed deeply. His nose could tell him far more than his eyes.

He was immediately overwhelmed by the stench of Ankle Snap Alley. He could barely smell any of his prey. There were hints of squirrel and mouse and rat and fox and stoat and skunk on the wind, but none of that particularly musky scent of raccoon.

Most of what he smelled was garbage.

There was the sickly sweet smell of rotting meat and the heavy stench of moldy vegetables. He could almost taste the bitter stink of rust and the tongue-tingling wet of old rags left too long in the rain. Food and waste and filth all mingled, and Titus longed for the comfort of his People's home, with the perfumed linens on the bed and a roasting chicken in the oven . . . but no!

No distractions now! He had to focus. The animals of Ankle Snap Alley were filthy flea-bitten vermin, and the stench was only further proof that they had to be expelled or destroyed. They would no longer pollute the civilized places of the world, not if Titus could do anything about it.

His second in command, a fast-talking hamster named Mr. Peebles, stood by Titus's side, gripping a book of matches to use as both shield and weapon. "You think they ran away, Titus?"

The dog smiled. He raised a delicate paw from the ground and licked between his toes. The army at his back watched him closely. "I think they fled from us," he said.

"You hear that?" Mr. Peebles shouted. "They fled from us! From the Flealess!"

"FLEALESS!" the army responded, brandishing their weapons in the air.

The assembled house pets had armed themselves with the best weaponry they could pilfer from their homes. There was a pit bull holding a giant chew toy in his mouth to use as a club. A Shetland sheepdog held a sock stuffed with a baseball, and two Siamese cats gripped a length of colorful ribbon between them, studded with thumbtacks. A parrot held a bag of chili powder to drop from the sky, and a large bearded lizard had fashioned herself a blow-gun. Her claws wrapped tightly around a straw, and she wore a quiver of sewing needles slung over her back.

In addition to all those weapons, the Flealess had the ancient tools of tooth and claw, well maintained and cared for by the People's kindly veterinarians.

"Careful, Titusssss." Basil slithered to the dog's side and whispered in his ear. "They are ssssneaky here."

"Don't worry, Basil," Titus told him. "You're on the

winning side now. Enjoy it."

Titus almost felt bad to see the mangy citizens of the alley go up against his army. It wasn't fair, of course, but let People worry about fairness. Animals worried about one thing and one thing alone: their turf.

A French bulldog snorted in anticipation. The tiny snub-nosed dog had armed himself with a board on wheels, a child's toy, that he intended to use as a battering ram, without having considered that such a toy wouldn't roll on the broken concrete and dirt of Ankle Snap Alley. "Maybe they're still here," he suggested. "Maybe they're hiding."

Titus smiled at the bulldog. He cocked his head to the side. Then he let out one bark, and Mr. Peebles flung himself onto the dog's head, scratching the space between its ears until the dog fell off his rolling board and cried for mercy.

"You do not question me," Titus shouted. "You simply obey. Understood?"

"Yes, sir," the army responded in a chorus of barks and whistles and hoots and yells.

"Good," said Titus. "Sixclaw! Report!"

The orange cat crept forward, his mouth clamped shut. When he stood before Titus, he neither saluted nor bowed nor provided any greeting of respect.

"Well?" Titus barked.

The cat spat out one small and terribly frightened news finch onto the ground.

"The coward heard my bell coming, and he spilled his guts before I could spill 'em for him."

Titus looked down at the terrified teen bird, his wings tied with a strand of dental floss and his tiny legs bound in a rubber band. "So? Do you want to go the way of the woodpecker, little finch? Speak! Are the vermin really gone?"

The finch ignored Titus and met Basil's eyes. "Chirp, chirp, chirp," said the bird, which even a house pet knew was a terrible insult from a finch.

Basil hissed and wrapped his coils around the news finch, but Sixclaw snatched it up with his claws, dangling the unfortunate animal above his open mouth.

"He's mine to eat, Basil," said Sixclaw. "Not yours."

"Chirp, chirp, chirp!" A flock of finches hiding in the tree above erupted.

"There we are," said Titus. "At least we know the finches stayed behind." He called up to the tree. "If you want your friend here to live, you will tell us the truth. Where are the others?"

The finches fell quiet. Titus had never known the news birds to fall quiet. The hair on his back bristled.

"You may eat the finch," he told Sixclaw.

"Wait! I'll tell ya," a pigeon cooed from beneath a

broken pail lying upside down on a dirt heap. Blue Neck Ned strutted out from his hiding spot and approached the army. "They got a secret plan, see, cooked up by that young raccoon, Kit. Thinks he's slicker than sunlight, that one does . . . but Blue Neck Ned's got his number, all right."

"Chirp, chirp, chirp," cursed the little finch dangling over Sixclaw's mouth again.

"Oh, hush up," said Blue Neck Ned. "I'm saving your beak, after all. We birds of a feather got to stick together."

"Talk," Titus ordered.

"Well, see, I ain't talking out of the goodness of my heart," Blue Neck Ned explained. "I wants me some of that good People food. I want a deal like Basil got."

"You want to become a house pet?" Titus laughed. "People do not keep pigeons for pets. You're too . . . filthy."

"Then I want fresh bread left out for me every day for a year, served to me real nice on a platter . . . by a cat in uniform."

"A cat serving a bird? Never!" A wave of muttering meows passed through the feline members of Titus's pack, but he silenced them with a quick bark.

"Deal," said the dog.

Sixclaw frowned.

"Well, then, what you need to know is this." Blue Neck Ned preened his feathers. "I never liked that little raccoon or his no-goodnik uncle, but they weren't no cushy Flealess house pets neither. They're cleverer than you. They sent this finch out to confound you and to delay you and then they sent me out to talk your ear off. All the meanwhile, they was laying in an ambush."

"An ambush?" Titus looked around, seeing no sign of an ambush. The dogs in his pack sniffed the air, but still, all they smelled was garbage.

"Problem you have," continued Ned, "is that you think we Wild Ones are at one another's throats all the time, we can't work together, but that's the way it goes with a community, see? We don't have to like one another to get along. Fact is, I don't like this here finch much neither, but I come all the way out to risk my blue neck to save his brown one, because he's my neighbor and that's what neighbors do."

"You haven't saved anyone," said Titus.

"Not yet," said Blue Neck Ned. "But now I have!"

With a sudden flap of his wings, Ned was in the air and he snatched the finch from Sixclaw's grasp, flitting above the cat's claws as fast as he could. At the same instant, all the news finches in the tree declared:

"Extra! Extra! Flealess Got Fooled!"

On the rooftops above the alley, a flock of pigeons assembled around Ned, all munching frantically on breadcrumbs. Behind them, Mrs. Costlecrunk and her hens sat on piles of acorns ready for flinging.

From the roof of the Rascals' van beside the Flealess, a troop of church mice appeared, wearing camouflage robes and armed with rubber band catapults and sharpened pencil spears.

Straight behind Titus, blocking the entrance to the alley, was a gaggle of creatures, rabbit and rat and ferret and stoat, rooster and frog and mangy dog, and in the front of this motley band was Kit, his front arms poking through tin cans he'd fashioned into armor, his hat tipped back on his head, and his eyes locked square on the eyes of his enemy.

"But how—?" Titus wondered. He hadn't smelled any of this army. They'd been hiding all around him, and he'd not caught the slightest scent. That's when he realized . . . those clever creatures stank up the alley on purpose. It was a trick!

Sixclaw whipped out the pouch that held Martyn and pulled the church mouse out, waving him in the air in front of Kit's army.

"You forget I've still got another hostage," said Sixclaw.

"Forget about me!" shouted Martyn. "I only regret that I have but one life to give for mousekind!"

"He knows we're not all mice, right?" Eeni whispered to Kit.

Kit shrugged. "We're all of one claw to him." He turned his attention to the Flealess horde. "No one's giving their lives today, brave scribe. Surrender now, Flealess, and you can go home to your masters. Surrender and live. The alley's big enough for us to share."

"Never!" shouted Mr. Peebles, striking a match and raising the flame into the air.

The Flealess army howled in response. They charged.

As the Flealess rushed forward, Kit almost lost his nerve. Basil slithered across the broken ground like a lightning bolt cutting the sky. The dogs leaped like crashing waves, and the cats cut the air like switchblades.

Kit stumbled backward at the sight, but Eeni touched his paw and gave him an encouraging nod.

"It's a good plan," she said. "And it's time to do it."

Kit nodded. He stepped forward, raised a paw in the air, and let slip his bark of war: "Aooooo!"

The battle for Ankle Snap Alley had begun.

Chapter Twenty-Seven

THE BARK OF BATTLE

AS the Flealess attacked in a solid wall of fur and scale and feather, the squirrels perched high atop the Gnarly Oak Apartments chattered their teeth against the heavy black power line that ran between the People's buildings. With great care and tremendous speed, they gnawed through it, and the line fell. It crashed to the ground in front of the advancing army with a flash of spark and flame.

The electric current popped against the earth; the line snaked and danced and cut the Flealess charge short. The house pets skittered and tried to dodge the sizzling wire. Those in the lead of the attack yelped as the sparks singed their fur, and a particularly unfortunate tabby cat who'd covered his paws in metal nails found himself unable to break free of the electricity.

"Ahh!!" he hissed as his fur fried around him. The pit bull with a giant chew toy in his mouth smacked the tabby sideways, knocking him free of the shocks, but also knocking the cat unconscious in the process.

The houses and streetlights and all the People's things that pulled electricity from that line went dark. People walking past on the sidewalks of the city stopped to listen to the great clamor of hoots and barks and screeches that accompanied the plunge into powerlessness.

Perhaps they thought it quaint how nature intruded on their city life, how the animals made their funny noises just as the power went out. They had no idea that on the other side of their buildings—in the rough-and-tumble alley where they dared not go themselves—the battle for the fate of the wild was raging.

In the chaos the electric wire caused, Martyn opened his little jaws wide and bit down on Sixclaw's sixth claw as hard as he could.

"Yoowww!" Sixclaw hooted as Martyn jumped free of his clutches, scurrying across the battlefield toward his faithful acolytes.

"Go, Strike Force," Kit yelled. "Strike!"

Seeing their leader was free, the church mice atop the van launched their catapults on the panicked Flealess army, pelting them with rocks and seeds and nuts.

The bearded lizard raised her blowgun to her lips to take out Martyn with a well-aimed needle, only to find the straw suddenly snatched from her claws by an arm that shot up from the dirt below. The ground in front of her quaked, and a cadre of moles burst up, hauling armfuls of rocks. The first mole turned the straw around on the lizard and pointed it between her eyes.

"Best be fleeing now, you cold-blooded monster," the mole said.

The lizard ran backward so fast, she tripped over her own tail and got her head stuck in the broken bicycle wheel. She kept running home, with no idea what her People would think when they had to pry the wheel off her that evening.

"Regroup! Attack!" Titus shouted to his chaotic horde before they all fled the field of battle.

"Air assault! Let 'em fly!" Kit yelled, and the pigeons took to the air, along with the finches, owls, and any other birds who'd grown tired of their friends and family becoming snack food for overfed outdoor cats.

Their droppings coated the Flealess, blinding them and making the ground slick with filth.

"Disgusting!" the pit bull with the giant bone yelled. He dropped his bone and tried to lick the bird droppings off his own tail, chasing himself in circles. A hail of acorns rained upon him from the hens of the roof.

"At them!" Titus commanded, and the Flealess air force of parrots and parakeets and one well-trained starling burst into the sky to meet the wild birds. Talon clashed with talon and beak with beak as the birds drew blood.

"Ground assault!" Kit yelled. "Charge!"

And the animals of Ankle Snap Alley charged.

The Blacktail brothers ran at the pit bull with the big chew toy. They ran side by side in armor made from discarded paperback books. Shane had a pawful of sharp can lids to throw, and Flynn had a fork and knife. He slashed and whirled and sent his foes running. The big pit bull charged to meet the brothers, matching them blow for blow and snarl for snarl.

Enrique Gallo strutted into the fray, his razor-sharp talons flashing this way and that. He cut through the studded clothesline held by the Siamese cats, who spun on him and tried to sink their claws into his back. He pecked himself free just as Mr. Peebles struck his match to singe the rooster's feathers. Enrique jumped the thrusting flame, the hamster missed, and the porcupine called the Teacher stabbed a quill through the little matchbook, swiping it away.

"En garde," said the porcupine.

"Eek!" said the disarmed hamster.

Possum Ansel and Otis the badger fought side by side. Ansel blinded an attacking terrier with a handful of sunflower salt, while Otis laid the terrier flat with one massive punch. A red-furred Persian cat with fresh finch on his breath snuck up behind them and bit Ansel's neck, making him fall frozen where he lay.

"You lay off my possum," Otis roared, and clubbed the cat so hard with a trash can lid that the cat's paws sank three inches down into the concrete. Ansel popped up again to his feet. The cat did not.

"Show no mercy to the filthy vermin," Titus yelled.

"Trying, General T! Aieee!" Mr. Peebles squeaked out. He was being chased in circles by the porcupine and yelping every time a quill poked him in the backside.

Basil raced for the old turtle, whom he found resting by the door to the van.

"Ssssorry, Bossss," said the snake. "But I'm the bossss now."

He struck, but the turtle simply vanished into his shell. Basil smacked his nose into the dirt. He whipped his body around and coiled himself over the turtle shell, squeezing as hard as he could, but to no effect.

From inside his shell, the turtle calmly called out, "I've outlived more snakes than you will ever meet in your life, Basil. You should never have betrayed the Rascals."

"Nope, certainly not," added Flynn, standing behind Basil now.

"Bad move, indeed," said Shane, beside his brother.

Before Basil could uncoil from the turtle to attack them, they'd jumped on their former partner in crime with their blades flashing. Flynn's fork pinned the snake's tail into the dirt, as Shane sent a can lid sailing at his head. Basil dodged it and then another and one more after that. They clattered off the side of the van behind him.

Distracted by the attack, Basil didn't see the turtle pop from his shell until it was too late to dodge a punch in the face that sent him sprawling on his back.

"Ugh!" he grunted, as his body pulled against the fork jabbed into his skin. He wiggled but couldn't free himself. The boss stood over him.

"Now that we've got a prisoner . . . ," said the turtle. "Perhaps I should call the teacher over for a lesson."

"Forget thissss!" Basil cried and, with a wiggle and twist, shed his skin, sliding away from his old friends by darting beneath the van and racing from Ankle Snap Alley.

"Good riddance!" Shane yelled after him.

"And don't come back!" Flynn added.

"Good job, boys," said the boss. "Now get back in the fight and show those prissy pets the meaning of pain."

The raccoon brothers bounded back into the battle.

Titus stood behind his army, watching the fight unfold. Across the battlefield, he locked eyes with Kit. He snarled and pawed at the dirt, then bounded straight in the pesky raccoon's direction.

Even though the gray dog was small and thin, he looked bigger than any other creature as he ran across the alley. His eyes were possessed by the madness of war; his jaws snapped this way and that. He bit the stoat and tossed him aside like a chew toy that'd lost its stuffing. He clamped his teeth down on the frog in the fur-trimmed coat and then trampled him underfoot, before the frog could mutter so much as a "heyo!"

"The lad's mine!" Sixclaw yelled, when he saw Titus running at Kit. The cat tossed three moles aside with one terrible swipe of his claw. "I want the head!"

"What is with you and your heads?!" Titus yelled back at him.

They ran, and as they ran, hidden traps sprang around them, but the two beasts moved so fast, so nimbly, that the traps snapped shut only on empty air in their wake.

Snap, snap, snap echoed off the high houses.

Squawk! Squawk! Squawk! cried the battling birds above.

Fighting animals snarled and barked all around.

"What now?" Kit wondered, as the dog and the cat rushed at him. Eeni and Uncle Rik still stood by his side.

"Well, there's the oldest tradition our kind has," Uncle Rik said.

"What's that?" Kit wondered, hoping it didn't involve him getting torn apart by a dog and a cat.

"An old-fashioned brawl," said Uncle Rik.

"I've never brawled before," said Kit.

"Well," Eeni instructed him, "the most important thing to remember is this: Don't get killed."

"Uh . . . thanks?" Kit flexed his claws. He'd never been in a fight in his life. He liked to win with wits and words. He wished he could think of a thing to say to stop *this* fight . . . but it was his words that had started it in the first place.

"Don't worry, Kit." Uncle Rik held his paw up. "We're fighting right beside you. Howl to snap."

"Howl to snap," added Eeni.

"For the Wild Ones!" Uncle Rik yelled, then charged forward to meet the little gray dog, whose jaws were wet with slobber and red with blood.

"For the Wild Ones!" yelled Eeni, charging after him.

"For my parents!" yelled Kit, and raced into the fray, his eyes fixed firmly on the six-clawed cat.

The bloodlust that overtook Kit as he ran wasn't a pretty feeling, and it wasn't nice, but the wild places of this world aren't always pretty and they aren't always nice. Kit was an animal after all, and he was about to unleash his wild side.

Chapter Twenty-Eight

CLAWS UP

WHILE Uncle Rik fought his way toward Titus, Kit scurried and weaved through the fight toward the orange cat.

He dove between the legs of the stray dog, Rocks, struggling to wrench the pit bull's chew toy from his grasp. The skunk from Larkanon's sprayed the pit bull straight in the face with his stench.

"Aw, disgusting," the pit bull cried, dropping the toy. "First bird poop? Now skunk spray? I'm going home!"

The pit bull left the battle, bruised, bloodied, and stinking.

Kit couldn't see Sixclaw anymore. He scanned the

fracas for a flash of orange fur, but saw none. Two dogs in brightly colored collars had a fox in a three-piece suit pressed against a wall by the neck, where they took turns ramming him in the stomach with their heads and laughing. Mr. Peebles was now fighting the teacher with one of the porcupine's own quills, matching him jab for jab and poke for poke.

In other spots, outdoor cats had stepped on traps and the mice had taken them prisoner. Dogs fled from rabbit punches, and the pigeons had sent the parrots flying south early. Kit couldn't tell who was winning the battle and who was losing, such was the chaos of fur and feather before him.

But then he saw Eeni, high in the air, slung over the back of the bright orange cat, who was carrying her away toward the fence and the train tracks below.

He glanced over to where his uncle was fighting Titus. Otis and Ansel had joined him, the three of them against the one miniature greyhound, but the small gray dog whirled and knocked them back with paws and teeth. He kicked the badger between the eyes, snapped his jaws at the possum, and whacked Uncle Rik sideways with his tail.

"Nice try, vermin!" the little dog taunted. "But I've studied with the greatest claw-jitsu masters in the world." He jumped and knocked Ansel into Otis, then flipped Uncle Rik onto his back. "Ha-ha!" he cried.

"Ahh!" Kit heard Eeni's scream.

"Go!" Uncle Rik panted, lifting himself to his feet and spitting the blood from his snout. "We'll keep this mutt busy."

"Who are you calling a mutt, ringtail?" Titus snarled. "I'm a purebred, and you're worm food!"

"Come at me!" Uncle Rik barked, and Titus charged.

At the fence over the train tracks, Sixclaw stopped. The cat carefully bound Eeni to the wire with twist ties at her wrists and ankles. He ran a claw under her chin and he smiled. "Let's just see how clever your friend is now, shall we?"

Eeni spat in the cat's face. "You're a hairball with fangs!"

The cat blinked his bright yellow eyes and licked the spittle off his nose. "Well, you're just a filthy white rat who's going to be forgotten as soon as she's been eaten. Not even your mommy will cry for you."

Eeni flinched as if she'd been punched. Sometimes the worst wounds came from words, not claws.

The cat grinned. "Oh yes, I know all about you," he whispered into Eeni's ear. His face loomed giant next to hers. "The eldest girl of your family always joins the Rat King. An unbroken chain from your mother and your grandmother all the way back as far as memory goes.

Except you broke that chain. You dropped out of school, refused to volunteer, and now, unlike any daughter in your family before you, you will die all alone . . . just as soon as I kill that pesky raccoon pal of yours."

"Well, you better hurry up," said Kit, catching his breath. "Because we haven't got all day to wait for you."

The cat turned to face him.

"Let my friend go," said Kit. "And we can settle this."

"We can settle this even if I don't let your friend go," said Sixclaw. "You forget, you have nothing to offer me but your life, and that I plan to steal."

"You can't steal what's freely given," said Kit, opening his paws wide in a gesture of surrender. "Let her go, and you can do with me what you please."

"Kit, no!" cried Eeni.

Kit nodded. "Too many innocent creatures are getting hurt."

"But you can't sacrifice yourself," said Eeni. "You're my friend."

"I'm your friend," said Kit, "so I have to. But please, Eeni, do me a favor when I'm gone?"

"What favor?" Eeni asked, stifling a sob.

"Please, stay out of the sewers," Kit said. "Gayle's still hungry, and it's not safe there. I told her I'd ring the dinner bell when it was time to eat . . . and I haven't yet."

He winked at Eeni.

"So, please," he pleaded. "Don't go in the sewers."

Eeni nodded. "Okay, Kit, I promise. I won't go in the sewers."

"Adorable," said Sixclaw. "Friendship among vermin."

The cat untied Eeni, then picked her up by her neck, pinched between his claws, about to let her go.

But he did not let her go. He laughed, and the little bell around his neck tinkled as he laughed.

Kit tensed.

"You see, I don't want you to surrender, Kit," Sixclaw said. "I want the thrill of the kill. I'm a cat, after all. That's what I do. I kill vermin."

He lifted Eeni up higher and held her over the sewer grate.

"Please, sir," Kit pleaded. "No matter what you do, don't drop her into the sewers with the hungry alligator."

"Oh, well, when you ask me that way . . ." Sixclaw laughed and, with a flick of his wrist, tossed Eeni down the drainage grate into Gayle's sewer.

"Ahh!" Eeni yelled, but she winked at Kit as she fell. The cat didn't even notice her quick pickpocket paws snatching his collar off as she flew. The bell dinged once before she and it were silenced in the darkness below.

"Now let's do our dance," Sixclaw hissed.

With his back paw, he kicked a cloud of dirt into Kit's face and, at the same instant, sprang on him. Kit was knocked backward to the ground, the cat on top of him. He could feel the pinpricks of the sharp claws piercing his fur. He tried to knock the orange cat off, but Sixclaw was too strong for him. The cat tried to bite at Kit's wrists, but the cans he wore as armor protected him. Kit took a swing with one of them and bashed Sixclaw across the head. That knocked the cat sideways and let Kit twist himself free. He popped to his feet.

But he wasn't a trained fighter, and Sixclaw was.

"Claws up, Kit!" he heard a news finch shout. "Keep your claws up!"

Before Kit could raise his claws, though, the cat was on him, tackling him facedown and pressing his snout into the dirt.

"You know, when I sent those dogs to kill your parents, I didn't expect you to run away," Sixclaw taunted. Kit's nose squished against the ground. He couldn't breathe. The cat's claws cut deeper into him. He felt blood trickling down his side. "A good son wouldn't have run away. A good son would've stayed and fought. I was surprised, Kit, that you were *not* a good son. But I guess that's how you ended up here, in Ankle Snap Alley, where the most wretched vermin under all the skies go to die!"

Kit twisted his neck around to see the cat on his back, silhouetted now by the white-hot sun above him. The cat had one claw raised, preparing to swipe and slash Kit's neck open. No matter how Kit struggled, he couldn't free himself.

Behind the cat, he saw the Blacktail brothers. They were out of breath from fighting, but they were still armed and close enough to help him. They would never be his friends, but they were on the same side in this battle at least.

Even as the air was leaving his lungs, Kit found the strength to call out. "Help!" he cried. "Shane! Flynn! Help me!"

The Blacktail brothers looked at Kit in his peril, looked at each other, and simply turned away.

Indifference was *their* revenge.

Kit closed his eyes. He pictured his mother and father in their burrow back beneath the Big Sky, and he smiled. He would see them again soon. Let the struggles of the wide world work themselves out. He could feel the fight leaving him. Even the sunlight felt cooler all of a sudden, like it was turning into the Forever Moonlight, where all raccoons go when their time has come. Kit would miss his new friends in the alley, but now, at least, he was going home.

"Do it quickly," he whispered to Sixclaw.

"Wait!" Titus shouted. Kit opened his eyes and saw the small gray dog standing atop a trash can at the other end of the fence. Otis and Ansel, Rocks the dog, and Uncle Rik were all tied up at its base. Enrique Gallo, the mighty rooster, talons dripping with the blood of the Flealess, had also fallen. He lay, wheezing with a wounded wing, against the Dumpster at the entrance to the alley, held in place by twin German shepherd dogs in spiked collars. Titus shouted loud enough that even the birds in the sky stopped flapping their wings. The fighting petered out all around. The alley fell quiet; only the whines and whimpers of wounded animals sliced the silence.

"You have fought well, vermin of Ankle Snap," Titus announced. "But you have lost. Behold your hero, there!" He pointed at Kit on the ground. "Surrender and we will allow you to go into exile. Head out from this place, go wherever you vermin go, and never return to the turf beneath the Slivered Sky, and then, you will live. But if you stay and fight, we will kill you all, as surely as we'll kill this raccoon."

Titus waited.

And then, the skunk lowered his tail, hung his head, hiccupped once, and turned away. He staggered from the alley without another word.

Kit watched as a family of foxes slipped from their hidey-hole and scampered off in broad daylight. The moles grumbled in their own old language, then vanished into the ground to tunnel to less dangerous dirt. A squirrel whispered to another squirrel, and the whisper was passed along, and every squirrel in the alley ran to pack their seeds and nuts.

"They're smarter than they look," said Titus.

"No more waiting," Sixclaw whined. "I want to kill him now!"

"One thing first," said Titus, hopping down from the trash can and prancing over to Kit on his spindly gray legs. "I want to know, Kit, if you really believed you could win? Did you actually think that all these winged, wattled, furred, and feathered vermin belonged here together? Did you really think you could unite them?"

Kit did his best to shrug, but couldn't move much beneath the cat. Instead of answering, he just rolled his eyes around the alley. Titus followed his gaze. The wounded animals, mole and mouse and pigeon and rat alike, helped one another grab what they could carry and close their shops to go into exile. On the field of battle, there were injured stoats nursing bleeding ferrets. Mrs. Costlecrunk, the gossiping chicken, held the hand of the fox in his bloody suit, and an owl stood among the church mice, advising them on the best way to bandage their wounds.

"Wind the cloth in a counter-centrifugal motion, chaps! *Counter*-centrifugal!" the owl hooted while the mice smiled politely and acted like they understood him.

"I never could have united them," said Kit. "But it looks like you did it for me. By trying to destroy us, you turned us into a community. I guess sometimes it takes a villain to show everyone else how to be a hero."

Titus growled, snarled, and barked at the insult. "Kill him!" he shouted at Sixclaw. "I changed my mind! Kill them all! Let none escape this alley!"

"With pleasure." Sixclaw smiled.

"You should have been more circumspect," Kit said with his last ounce of breath.

"Circum-what?" the cat wondered, but Kit didn't have time to answer. Sixclaw swiped his claws toward Kit's throat.

Chapter Twenty-Nine

A DEAL'S A DEAL

THE cat's claws never touched Kit. There was a *SNAP!* so loud it shook the ground.

"No," Titus yelled. "Impossible!"

Kit looked up just in time to see Gayle let out a voluminous burp as she hit the ground. On the alligator's back sat a white rat, riding her into the heart of the Flealess horde and holding Sixclaw's belled collar dinging in the air.

The Flealess shrieked and scattered.

"It's Gayle!" they yelled. "She's left the sewers!"

The army fell into a full retreat before the gator's teeth.

"Thanks for keeping your promise, Kit," Gayle told Kit. "That cat was delicious."

"I thought we agreed there would be no revenge," Uncle Rik said.

"There wasn't," said Kit. "Sixclaw rang his own dinner bell when he tossed Eeni down there."

"Smart move, Kit," said Eeni. "Getting Sixclaw to throw me down into the sewers."

"I'm only as smart as the friends I count on," said Kit. "And it helps when they can snatch the collar off a killer cat."

"Well, you can always count on me when something needs snatching," said Eeni.

"Howl to—"

SNAP!

Gayle snapped her jaws at Titus, who was trying to hop away. He took a clumsy step, and a wire trap popped up around him. "Ahh! I'm stuck," he yelled.

"So, Kit," Gayle asked. "You want me to eat this dog? He looks cleaner than most of the snacks I get."

"No, please, no . . . ," the small dog pleaded, his voice suddenly as high and yippy as one would expect from a dog of his breeding. "Kit, please . . . don't let her eat me! I just want to go back home!"

Kit looked at Titus, quivering in the cage, helpless in

front of the giant reptile. As helpless as Kit's own mother had been when the pack of hound dogs came for them.

"I could let you go . . . ," said Kit, "*if* you recognize that the Bone of Contention grants the Wild Ones the right to live in this alley from now on. And swear before the scribes that the Flealess will let us live here in peace. Do that, and I'll ask Gayle not to eat you."

Titus whimpered, but nodded.

Gayle shrugged. "I was full anyway."

Martyn stepped forward, writing quill and bark in hand. "The scribes are ready," he declared, and Titus inked his shaking paw through the wire of the cage and pressed it down onto a new agreement for peace between the Flealess and all the families of fur and paw, wing and claw who chose to call Ankle Snap Alley home from that moment forward until the last moonbeam touched the world.

"Lousy flea-bitten den of filth," Titus muttered when he made his mark. "You can have it. Now let me out of this cage!"

Kit ignored Titus. Let the People free their own pets, he decided. Maybe it would teach them to be more careful where they put their traps.

"Kit, would you do the honors?" Martyn asked, extending the ink to him.

Kit dipped his paw and then, like Azban, the First Raccoon, he pressed it to the bark to seal the deal on behalf of all the Wild Ones. The crowd erupted in cheers. They hoisted him and Eeni and Uncle Rik onto their backs and paraded them through the battle-torn wreckage of Ankle Snap Alley.

"Why are they cheering for me?" Uncle Rik wondered. "I'm an historian. Historians don't get carried away. Put me down!"

The creatures laughed, and no one paid any attention to Titus in his cage.

"Let me out," he shouted. "Hey!"

The creatures of Ankle Snap Alley were bloody and battered, but laughing and making music with every hoot and howl and flap and whistle their voices could produce.

"What now?" Kit wondered as they set him down. Every creature under the Slivered Sky seemed to want to shake his hand.

"The finches will want to interview you," Eeni told him. "And the Blacktail brothers won't have forgiven you. And who knows what that Titus will think up next. He's whipped, but I bet he's not beaten."

"So this isn't over yet, is it?" Kit sighed.

"The only things that ever really end are rainbows and summer naps," said Eeni.

"What'll we do if they come back, though?" Kit

wondered. "What if they ignore our deal again?"

"We don't need their permission to stay," Eeni reminded him. "We're wild. We hold our ground. Together."

"Yeah," said Kit. "We do."

Chapter Thirty

WILD LIFE

THE turn and tumult of life returned to Ankle Snap Alley. Ansel and Otis cleaned up their bakery, repaired the counter, and brought in new trash-can lids for tabletops. They reopened once more to serve hungry creatures who had a few extra seeds in their pockets to spend on candied corn husks and jelly-stuffed banana peels. They did add one new item to the menu, in honor of the great Siege of Ankle Snap Alley: sweet-'n'-spicy cat paw stew.

Blue Neck Ned's eyes bulged when he saw it on the menu. In the kitchen, Otis laughed.

"Relax, Ned," Ansel told the pigeon. "There's no real

cat paw in there. It's just leftover cat food the Rabid Rascals sell from the Dumpster."

"I knew that," Blue Neck Ned grumbled, before digging into a piping-hot bowl of the stuff.

The air was turning crisp, hinting at winter, and all the creatures were doing their best to pack on extra fat before the lean months to come. They'd sometimes glance at the lighted windows of the People's homes and wonder who had the better deal, the free and wild vermin of the alley or the cruel and coddled Flealess, who'd be warm and well fed for winter.

Shane and Flynn Blacktail set up their game again, this time near the Scavengers' Market, where the Rabid Rascals hung out, figuring they'd have protection if they needed it. Ever since Kit had rallied the animals to fight together, the Blacktail brothers had been nervous they'd turn on them next. They weren't about to play honest, so they needed to play near some muscle.

"An acorn here, a peanut there. If you pick your nose, you'll pick nose-hair," Flynn sang, although the ballyhoo wasn't his best and he had no takers that evening. The moles went to work, the chickens gossiped, and Enrique Gallo ran his barbershop.

Among it all, Kit felt at home.

"Good to see you, Kit, my lad," the skunk greeted him

on his way into Larkanon's. The skunk's name, it turned out, was Brevort. Rocks, the dog outside Larkanon's, never exactly said a kind word, but he'd lift his head and snort once if Kit walked by, which was for Rocks a great show of magnanimity.

"Mag-na-nimity?" Kit asked Eeni when she used the word.

"It's like generosity," Eeni explained.

"Why not just say 'generosity' then?" Kit wondered.

"Because where's the fun in that?" Eeni shook her head. "If everyone just said what they meant, talking wouldn't be any kind of trick at all."

"Talking shouldn't be any kind of trick at all!"

"Says you." Eeni laughed, and the two friends walked together paw in paw to find the trash can Uncle Rik had discovered to pilfer "historical artifacts."

"Scholarship doesn't cease," Uncle Rik called out from above, his rear end sticking straight up to the sky, with his voice muffled inside the can. "It offers new mysteries to the curious raccoon who seeks them! Wonderful mysteries!"

"What'd you find?" Kit asked him.

"It's the score of the season! We'll be wintering like walruses!" Uncle Rik began tossing his loot out of the trash can and over his head, so that Kit and Eeni had to scramble to catch the stuff to put it into the satchel they'd brought.

There were unraveled mittens and half-gnawed apple

cores. There were worn-out shoes that didn't match each other, and a variety of fruits that matched each other too well in moldy green.

"And something special for you, Kit," Uncle Rik declared, tossing up a strange little item, a strap with a buckle and a flat dial on it, ringed with People's writing.

"They call it a watch," said Uncle Rik. "They use it to tell the passage of time."

"They look at *this thing* to tell time?" Kit marveled. "Why don't they just look at the sky?"

Uncle Rik shrugged. "People play their own games, I guess . . . but that's filled with gears and springs and all kinds of parts. I thought you'd like to tinker with it."

"Thanks, Uncle Rik. I—"

Suddenly, they heard the loud *snap* of a trap in the distance. They all tensed, then relaxed when the sound was followed with the tiny whining voice of a mouse.

"Little help! Hello! I seem to have gotten myself stuck in this trap! Hellooo! Kit?"

It was Martyn, who managed to get himself trapped every other night. Kit had a nice little business springing animals out of the old traps that the People hadn't cleaned up, although they had stopped leaving new ones after they found their beloved Titus howling and shivering in one of them on a cool afternoon.

Kit's uncle insisted he should charge a fee for getting

the trapped animals out, but Kit usually ended up doing it for free. Most of the animals of Ankle Snap Alley couldn't afford to pay him anyway.

"I gotta go help the mouse." Kit sighed.

"You've a good heart," said Uncle Rik.

"Too good for this place," said Eeni.

Kit blushed. Eeni gave him a friendly push.

"I'll sure miss you two this winter," said Uncle Rik.

"Yeah, you wi— wait. What?" Kit cocked his head, tipped his hat back on his ears. "Why will you miss us? Where are you going?"

It was Eeni's turn to blush. Uncle Rik gazed down at her from the trash can. "You didn't tell him?"

She shook her head.

"But I thought you were going to—oh, chirping chickens, I'll do it." Uncle Rik cleared his throat. "Kit, you and Eeni are going to school."

"We are? But . . ."

"Saint Rizzo's Academy," said Uncle Rik. "A very fine place."

"It's all right," Eeni grunted.

"But I want to stay here," Kit whined.

"Eeni will be going too," Uncle Rik told him. "You need to be around creatures your own age. And you need an education. Ankle Snap Alley's no substitute for rigorous study."

"But . . . but . . ." Kit couldn't think of a reasonable objection, so he threw his arms in the air and shouted, "I'm wild!"

Uncle Rik shook his head. "We can talk about it tomorrow. Let's go to Ansel's and get some dinner. It's late and the sun will be coming up soon."

As they walked toward the bakery, Kit couldn't get over it. "School?" he said again. "Really?"

"Trust me, Kit." His uncle put a hand across his nephew's back. "It's a big world beyond the alley, and even the wildest of creatures still has a lot left to learn."

Turn the page for a sneak peek at the sequel!

Moonlight Brigade

Chapter One

MUSKY MO HEARS THE MUSIC

BRIGHT leaves fell from tired trees, and day by day they browned on the forest floor. Cool air sharpened its bite and nipped at the skin of any animal who hadn't begun to thicken his fur or fortify his feathers. Winter was on its way.

On a riverbank near the giant city of steel that the animal folk called the Slivered Sky, a gang of otters had gathered, huddling to keep warm, while the brittle ground crunched beneath their claws. They sat in front of a traveling coyote, who had an old tin-can guitar strapped to his back.

"If you think this winter will be cold, let me sing you a song of the real winters in the Howling Lands, where the sun shines but gives no warmth, where the lakes freeze over thicker than a turtle's shell, and a sneeze shatters when it hits the ground. These are the hungry winters and a fella without supplies surely goes cold and dies."

The coyote's voice was scary and soothing at the same time. It slid from his tongue like gravel coated in gravy. The otters held one another's paws as they listened to him.

"You ever sneezed an icicle?" the coyote asked.

The otters shook their heads no in awed silence.

"Want to hear a song about it?"

The otters nodded their heads yes.

No one had ever seen this gang of otters this quiet before. These were the Thunder River Rompers, twenty in all, and they considered themselves the toughest, tightest, and most terrible of all the river otter gangs around.

Weren't they the ones who knocked over the big Beaver Dam three seasons back?

Yep, sure as sunshine, they were.

Weren't they the ones who chased off a full-grown hawk just this past summer?

Everyone knew they were, especially that frightened hawk.

Weren't they the gang that rumbled and raised a ruckus with any passing creature, and considered themselves the only pals o' the paw worth palling around with anyway?

Yep, that was the Thunder River Rompers, best of brothers and brawling-est of beasts.

So why *were they sitting here, drop jawed and wide-eyed, listening to some mangy coyote tell a tall tale instead of pounding him into the dirt, flaying his fur, and using his pelt to cozy up their riverbank holts?*

That was the question their leader, Musky Mo, put forward with a snarl, just as the coyote was about to start his song.

"I could use a coyote-fur couch this winter," Musky Mo said. "Looks mighty warm to me!"

The coyote sat back on his haunches and looked the leader of the otters over lengthways and long ways and up ways and down ways. He had a smirk on his gray muzzle and a devious twinkle in his eye. There were scars that cut through the brown-and-gray fur on his back and he wore not a stitch of clothes.

Even the otters, freer than any folk, wore wrist cuffs woven from seaweed and green knit watch caps with their gang insignia emblazoned on the front: a terrible otter claw bursting from a frothy river, a fish in its fist.

They also wore glasses, every one of them, because when otters were on land, they were nearsighted.

Once, a passing skunk shouted that the Thunder River Rompers were more like Thunder River Rubes. The skunk had a good stinking laugh over that, because a rube was a foolish fellow. Musky Mo, never one to let an insult pass, dragged that skunk into the river and held him down so long, he washed the stink right off him. No one had ever disrespected the Thunder River Rompers after that.

But the coyote didn't seem to care a whisker for the Rompers, or Musky Mo's reputation as a drowner of skunks. He'd stepped from the dark brush and settled himself in front of them without so much as a "beg your pardon," and then he'd offered to start singing songs like the riverbank was his very own turf.

Musky Mo was not having it. "So how about you get up out of here, coyote, before I make it so you can't never get up from anywhere again."

Coyote liked his winter song and *did not* like to be interrupted when he was about to sing it. Confronted with Musky Mo's demand that he "get up out of here," the coyote licked his lips.

"I didn't mean to bother you fine fellows," the coyote said, the gravel in his voice getting rougher. "I know you otter folk have a lot of ruckus to raise before winter sinks her teeth in. I'm only a weary traveler seeking some rest and some good company. I'll be off shortly. But first, perhaps, might I sing my song?"

"You're not welcome here," Mo grunted at him, flexing his webbed front paws for a fight. "And none of us want to hear your howling. Right, boys?" He grimaced to show off his otter fangs. The rest of the gang stood up behind him and grunted.

The coyote was bigger than all of them, but grossly outnumbered. He sighed as he swung the guitar off his back. "Why don't I play you just one song before I go? It's a short song."

Musky Mo laughed when he saw the guitar. "You ain't got no strings on your guitar," he said, pointing. The other otters laughed along with their leader, because indeed, the coyote's tin-can guitar didn't have a single string on it. "What good's a guitar without any strings? It won't make a sound!"

"Well, you best listen closely then," the coyote said, and began to strum the invisible strings. The otters stopped laughing and furrowed their brows at this strange coyote. Perhaps he had Foaming Mouth Fever? He wasn't actually foaming at the mouth, but he was acting stranger than any canine the Thunder River Rompers had ever come across.

The coyote plucked and played his stringless guitar with passion, closing his eyes and tapping his back paws, nodding along to a tune that only he could hear.

After a moment, he opened his eyes and looked at the dumbfounded gang of otters. "Ya like my song, boys?"

"We don't hear nothin'," Musky Mo grumbled.

"Listen a little closer," the coyote said. "I wrote this song for you Rompers, after all."

The otters leaned forward to listen closer, bending their thick necks and lowering their little heads toward the guitar. Their tiny ears twitched in anticipation of the music.

The coyote looked down at his audience and adjusted his grip on the musical instrument . . . and then he turned it around and smashed its heavy end down onto Musky Mo's head!

He flattened the otter's face into the cold mud with a *splat*, then swung the guitar along the line of other otters, knocking them into one wet otter heap.

"*Ooof! Ooof! Ooof!*" they grunted.

Musky Mo tried to get up and grab the coyote's tail, but the coyote jumped away, tossing his stringless guitar as he spun. The guitar knocked three more Thunder River Rompers back into the mud, and the coyote landed behind Musky Mo. Before the otter could turn around, the coyote lifted Musky Mo off the ground by the scruff of his neck and faced him toward his own gang.

The otter's paws scrambled uselessly in the air and the coyote grinned through clenched teeth. Musky Mo's eyes widened as his gang froze in place, unsure how to help their boss.

The coyote shook his head ferociously and flung Musky Mo head over tail into the Thunder River.

"Swim away, Musky Mo!" the coyote yelled after him. "If I see your furry face again, I'll turn your bones to toothpicks!" Then he lowered his head and growled at the gang of otters whose leader he had just sent swimming. "I think you all need a new leader . . . unless you want to hear me sing again? I've got enough song in me for each and every one of you."

The otters were bruised and banged from the coyote's first song and had no desire to hear another. One by one, they brushed themselves off, put their busted glasses back on their faces, and, one by one, they opened their paws and lowered their heads to the coyote.

"We surrender," they said.

"What's your name?" one of the otters—a burly brute named Chuffing Chaz—looked up to ask, then lowered his snout back down toward the dirt.

"My name doesn't matter," the coyote told them. "You

can call me Coyote. And I welcome the Thunder River Rompers to my band."

"Band?" Chuffing Chaz asked.

"Oh yes," said Coyote, panting with glee. "You're my band. And together we'll make beautiful music."

The otters smirked, because they now knew what the coyote meant by *music*, and this time, they'd get to help him with the *singing*.

"Now," Coyote cleared his throat and picked his guitar up from the mud, "who can tell me which way it is to a place called Ankle Snap Alley? That's where we've got a concert to perform."

Chapter Two

PALS OF THE PAW

IT'S not right to be awake so early," Eeni grumbled. Her tiny pink nose sniffed the chilly air, while her tiny pink paws scrambled along the pavement to keep up with Kit. The dry leaves crackled under her toes, snapping with the season's first frost.

Kit had to slow down for Eeni because just one of his raccoon steps was about six steps for a rat of her size. He looked over at his small friend, whose complaining, he had learned, was part of her waking-up routine.

Some creatures did jumping jacks, some stretched or groomed themselves, while others took a moment to give thanks to their ancestors, to the ground, and to the sky.

Eeni, however, could not fully wake up until she had complained about something for at least two hundred steps across Ankle Snap Alley. She was a street-smart, runaway albino rat who was slick enough to pick a kangaroo's pocket, but she was *not* a rat who suffered in silence.

If she was going to wake up early, she was going to whine about it.

"The sun's barely started to set!" she declared. "It's too bright out! It's too cold! The hedgehogs are getting ready to hibernate! Why don't rats hibernate? Or raccoons? We should hibernate! We should *all* hibernate."

"Looks like some folks are starting early," Kit observed.

Across the way, Brevort the skunk lay sprawled on the ground, snoring and drooling onto the rock he was using as a pillow. His drool had frozen into a long icicle on his furry face. His quick breaths made misty clouds in the air in front him.

Kit and Eeni crossed the broken concrete to the side of the Dancing Squirrel Theater. They clambered over the old tires and broken bicycles that littered the alley, charged through whitewashed heaps of trash and freezing weeds that prickled and tickled their tummies, and they stood in front of the skunk. He lay on the ground just outside the door of a place where no self-respecting animal ever set claw or paw. It was called Larkanon's, and luckily for the stray dog who owned it, there weren't a lot of self-respecting animals in Ankle Snap Alley. He did a brisk business in cheese ale and moldy snack crackers.

The sleeping skunk had on a dirty pair of striped pants that matched the stripe down his back. He snored louder than a bear, and his tongue lolled out of his mouth. His pockets lolled out of his pants the same way. Some citizen of Ankle Snap Alley had emptied the sleeping skunk's pockets of every last seed and nut he had.

"Wake up, Brother Brevort." Kit nudged the skunk with a paw, using his other to hold his nose from the skunk's pickle-and-graveyard stench. The skunk groaned.

"The Bagman's coming!" Eeni shouted and Brevort sat bolt upright.

"Where? Where is he?" the skunk shouted. His tail shot up, ready to spray his stinky spray.

Eeni laughed and Brevort frowned. "That's a lousy trick," he grumbled. "Telling a sleeping fellow the Bagman's coming."

"It woke you up, didn't it?" Eeni said.

She knew it wasn't nice. Every animal in Ankle Snap Alley was afraid of the Bagman. He was the Person who came to empty the ankle-snapping traps when animals got caught in them. When a fella went into the Bagman's bag and went away, he never came back. Some animal folk wouldn't even joke about the Bagman.

But not Eeni. There was nothing off-limits to her sense of humor.

Brevort rubbed his head, only noticing then that he had a single acorn clutched in his paw. He stared at it like a snake studying a shoe.

"Time to go home," Eeni told him. "You've been robbed, but they left you an acorn. Use it to buy yourself breakfast."

"Or eat it *for* breakfast," Kit suggested.

"Oh." The skunk looked down at his pockets, not seeming the least bit surprised that they'd been picked bare. "It was kind of them to leave me this acorn."

On the trees above the alley there weren't many acorns left. Even now, so early in the evening, the squirrels were busy above, bringing the last ones down to deposit in the bank.

The skunk stood, brushed himself off, and tipped his hat to the children, although he was not wearing a hat. "See you at the First Frost Festival," he said.

"See you," Kit and Eeni replied. The skunk stumbled his wild way back into the dark door of Larkanon's and disappeared.

"How many times has he had his pockets picked?" Kit wondered.

"I dunno," Eeni said. "I stopped doing it to him when I

was just a little ratlet. No sport in robbing that fellow. You almost feel bad for him."

"Almost," said Kit. "But folks make sure he survives the winter."

"Howl to snap," Eeni said. She held up her little pink paw to Kit's big black one.

"Howl to snap," he agreed. These were the words of Ankle Snap Alley, and saying them told everyone that you came from there and not some cozy field or forest out under the Big Sky. Howl to snap meant that even though you came into the world with a howl, and most creatures from Ankle Snap Alley went out again with the snap of a trap, you knew it was what you did in between that howl and that snap that made you who you were.

Kit had lived in Ankle Snap Alley for the whole leaf-changing season, ever since he'd lost his parents to a pack of hunting dogs, and he knew that all the animals who didn't live here thought the alley was just a nest of no-good dirty-rotten garbage-scrounging liars and crooks.

In fact, the alley *was* a nest of no-good dirty-rotten garbage-scrounging liars and crooks, but it was *his* nest of no-good dirty-rotten garbage-scrounging liars and crooks. Sure, they'd steal from a fella, but they'd always leave an acorn in his paw after they took ten from his pockets. In Ankle Snap Alley, folks looked out for one another, even when they didn't get along. There were folks in Ankle Snap Alley who cared about Kit, and folks Kit cared about.

In short, it was home. From howl to snap.

"Evening, Kit!" Kit's uncle Rik called out to them from across the alley. When Kit had lost his parents, it was his uncle Rik who had taken him in, Uncle Rik who had invited Eeni into their home when she had nowhere else to go either, and Uncle Rik who had enrolled them both in school for the coming winter.

Rik was a fuzzled old raccoon, prone to excitement over obscure bits of ancient history, more likely to trade his last seeds for an old book than a hot meal, but he was kind and generous and in an all-too-wild world, a kind and generous raccoon was the best thing you could have on your side. Kit wouldn't mind at all if he grew up to be like his uncle.

Except for the big book collection. Who needed all those books?

Uncle Rik waved them over in front of Possum Ansel's Sweet & Best-Tasting Baking Company. Already, a motley crew of bleary-eyed animals were lining up for their sunset breakfast at the popular café.

There were three squirrels Kit recognized from the Dancing Squirrel Theater, two frogs from the Reptile Bank and Trust going over long scrolls of bark covered from end to end in writing, a young church mouse with a satchel full of pamphlets to hand out, a chipmunk in a tattered overcoat, a twitchy weasel with a briefcase filled to bursting, a company of moles in hard hats, a news finch in his press visor arguing with a loud starling about last night's rabbit boxing match, and a sullen-looking rabbit boxer with a black eye and swollen ear. At the front of the line, stood a pigeon named Blue Neck Ned, who had a way of cutting to the front of any line in the alley.

Uncle Rik ignored all the creatures waiting and thrust a piping-hot chew pie apiece into Kit's and Eeni's paws.

"Ansel made them specially for you for the first day of school," Uncle Rik told them. "Hazelnut crust stuffed with banana peel, fish bones, blue cheese, and candied worms! Eat up!"

Kit's mouth watered at the thought. "Are those fried rose petals on top?" Kit asked. Uncle Rik nodded. Possum Ansel was a genius in the bakery.

"Why should those kids get special pies?" Blue Neck Ned cooed. "I been waitin' here since the sun was up!" He pecked at the doorframe angrily. "Open up and give me *my* breakfast!"

The door swung open and a big badger glared down at the pigeon, his paws crossed over the apron he wore. If Possum Ansel was a genius at baking treats, his partner, Otis the badger, was a genius at breaking beaks.

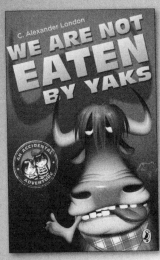